Minella struggled, kicking violently

"Stop that noise," Sam warned. "I'm not hurting you." When she cried even louder he silenced her by covering her mouth with his own.

Minella abandoned herself to the glorious turmoil that rushed through her body as he crushed her to him. If there was never another moment like this, she knew this one would never be forgotten.

Sanity returned as he dropped her on the bed, his eyes smoldering. "If you weren't so innocent, Minella, you'd know that's no way to stop a man doing anything. Quite the reverse."

She was rigid with the effort to control her anger and confusion.

"Isn't it enough that you've got Annette?" she blazed. "Do you collect women like scalps? You're not safe to be near. Now will you please go away!"

WELCOME
TO THE WONDERFUL WORLD
OF *Harlequin Romances*

Interesting, informative and entertaining,
each Harlequin Romance portrays an appealing
and original love story. With a varied array
of settings, we may lure you on an African safari,
to a quaint Welsh village, or an exotic Riviera
location—anywhere and everywhere that adventurous
men and women fall in love.

As publishers of Harlequin Romances, we're
extremely proud of our books. Since 1949,
Harlequin Enterprises has built its publishing
reputation on the solid base of quality and
originality. Our stories are the most popular
paperback romances sold in North America; every
month, six new titles are released and sold at
nearly every book-selling store in Canada and the
United States.

A free catalog listing all Harlequin Romances
can be yours by writing to the

HARLEQUIN READER SERVICE,
(In the U.S.) 1440 South Priest Drive, Tempe, AZ 85281
(In Canada) Stratford, Ontario, N5A 6W2

We sincerely hope you enjoy reading
this Harlequin Romance.

Yours truly,

THE PUBLISHERS
Harlequin Romances

The Candleberry Tree

Pamela Pope

Harlequin Books

TORONTO • NEW YORK • LONDON
AMSTERDAM • PARIS • SYDNEY • HAMBURG
STOCKHOLM • ATHENS • TOKYO • MILAN

Original hardcover edition published in 1983
by Mills & Boon Limited

ISBN 0-373-02573-4

Harlequin Romance first edition September 1983

CHAPTER ONE

THEY were rough with her when they hauled her on board the whaleboat. They thought she was drowned. When she coughed and struggled the men looked at each other in amazement and began to talk loudly in a language she didn't understand. Minella opened her eyes to try and see what they looked like. They wore bright jerseys and round black caps like French fishermen, but they were not French, and she wished she could remember whether they had been near any land when the storm struck. Nothing was clear at all.

'My name is Minella Farmer,' she said, her voice no more than a choking sound.

The boat tossed. Oars dug into waves which had lost much of their fury, but still rolled enough to make the going difficult. It was a miracle they had found her. The men shook their heads.

'My name . . . is. . . .' She wanted to tell them it again because it was the most important thing in the world, but this time she couldn't remember it, and her soft brown eyes closed wearily.

'*Inglesa.*' She caught the one word and sighed, deciding with relief that they must be Spanish. Not that it mattered what nationality they were. They had saved her life and she would love them forever.

She was aware of nothing more until the boat grounded on a rocky beach, grating loudly as it was dragged clear of the water, and there was a lot of shouting going on in the strange language. A small crowd had collected on the shore and the sun was shining. She didn't need to see it. The warmth was drying the salt water on her skin, making her lips parched and her eyelids too heavy to lift. Her limbs

were like lead, and the few clothes she had on clung to
her aching body. Someone had removed her lifejacket
and oilskins, and by the coarseness against her face she
guessed they were being used to cushion her head in the
bottom of the boat.

She wished she could remember what had happened,
but it brought a pain to her head when she tried. The
rocking had stopped, and she turned her head and
groaned as voices came closer. They gathered somewhere above her and curious people peered into the
whaleboat for a glimpse of this girl from the sea.

She was not conscious of anything except the hot sun
and the voices until she was picked up in the strongest
arms she had ever known and held against a broad
masculine chest. A blanket was wrapped round her, and
she realised the agitated sound in her ears had been her
teeth chattering, for in spite of the sun she was terribly
cold. The man made sure the blanket was tucked firmly
round, then set off up the beach with long, easy strides,
passing the voluble sightseers without a word. One
panting, puffing person tried to keep up with him, but
couldn't match the pace, and she smiled, hurting her
dry lips.

There was great strength in the man who carried her.
Though he walked quickly he didn't jolt her, and she
could feel the wetness of her clothes saturating his. He
climbed up, away from the shore, his soft-soled shoes
whispering over turf that was like carpet after the sand,
and at what must have been the top of the incline he
waited for his companion.

Minella felt him looking at her. For a moment he
was motionless; then he moved her head so that it
rested more comfortably against his shoulder, and
sensitive fingers stroked wet hair away from her face.
The fingers which lingered almost tenderly against her
cheek belonged to someone with rare perceptivity.

'You're like a little wet bird,' he said softly.

At first she hardly registered the fact that he had

spoken in English. The words had been a form of caress, like his gentle touch, and she was content to lie in his arms, feeling a wonderful warmth steal over her at last. She felt protected from the terror that had struck, as if she had come home, and this was where she wanted to stay.

Strange thoughts like these formulated in her mind, but made no sense.

There was a breeze blowing now they were higher up. She heard it catch at his shirt and set it billowing away from his back like a spinnaker. A sail. A jumble of memories cascaded through her mind like a kaleidoscope. She buried her face against his chest as fear swamped her with much the same force as the sea had done, and she cried out. It must have been the first sound she had made, because he touched her face again in sympathy. If only she could see what he was like!

'It's all right,' he murmured. 'You're safe now.'

Her eyelids refused to lift and her lashes fluttered on dry, burning cheeks, but through her lashes she had her first glimpse of the man who held her. It was nothing more than a general impression really, and her immediate conclusion was so silly she wondered if she was giggling. In her drowsy state she could imagine him stepping from the pages of the Arabian Nights tales she had loved when she was young.

She thought she asked him where she was, or who *he* was, but she couldn't have spoken the words aloud, because he gave no answer, or any indication that he had heard.

His trundling companion caught up with them, the panting increased with exertion, and they didn't speak. Minella found the effort of staying awake too great, and with a sigh she turned her head against the fresh-smelling shirt before drifting away on a wave of strange contentment.

Her next period of awareness was just as dramatic, but not quite so pleasant. This time she opened her eyes and looked round. She was in a small whitewashed room, a cubicle perhaps, and there was a bright light shining on her. The light hurt her eyes and she was glad when it was switched off so that only sunlight filtered through a tiny window. She was lying on a narrow bed, and a coloured blanket was wrapped round her like a cocoon, right up to her chin. She was very hot, and yet she still shivered.

She was not alone. There was a little man beside her and he was humming a tune. He had gentle fingers, but his touch was only sensitive to physical damage and he seemed to be a doctor. She guessed he was the one who had puffed up the hill behind them. She wondered where the tall man was, the one who had carried her. There had been communication between them on a level she didn't understand, and being a very active, practical girl who liked explanations for everything she was anxious to know that he was real. All she could remember was his shirt billowing out like a robe, dark curly hair and a bearded chin. Surely she hadn't imagined him entirely.

There was only the fat man in the room. Why wasn't her brother here looking after her? A surge of anxiety brought pain to her head, and muddled, half-formed pictures chased through her mind, making her toss on the pillow.

The doctor was bending over her when she looked up. He smiled, a quick, nervous smile that twitched the muscles of his face in rapid succession, and he was like a cuddly toy. Minella smiled back and he began to fuss over her excitedly.

'She is awake,' he called. Obviously there was someone not far away. 'Come and see what a pretty girl she is!'

'I'll take your word for it,' came the reply in a voice that sounded too indifferent to be the Englishman, yet she recognised the low, mellow ring. Surely he hadn't lost interest in her already.

'But, Sam——!' The fat man was agitated and spoke in heavily accented English. He hurried to the door. 'It is time you came and took her away. You know I cannot have her here all day. In an hour there will be patients to see me and I need the room. She will be better at your house. Sam, are you listening?'

Minella tried to sit up, struggling with the blanket, but her head was spinning and the walls closed in on her, forcing her back on to the hard bed. The little man came back quickly, clicking his tongue, and picked up a cup from a table beside the bed before slipping an arm beneath her shoulders and raising her head. The cup was put to her lips and warm liquid trickled down her throat. It wasn't tea or coffee. It tasted more like clear soup, and it warmed her deliciously.

'She is not hurt,' he called. 'No cuts or bruises. She is just very tired and shocked. Have you told the authorities she is here?'

The man called Sam didn't answer for several seconds. It was as if he was concentrating on something and didn't want to be disturbed.

Then: 'Not yet,' he said.

She wished she could see him, but everything had a dream quality. She seemed to be floating in a kind of bubble, looking down on what was happening but taking no part, like watching a play. But as the nourishment strengthened her she found the fragmented pictures in her mind staying longer in focus and began to remember things.

She remembered the yacht. She had been taking part in a race across the Atlantic, crewing for some friends of her brother.

'Perhaps there are other survivors,' the fat man was saying.

It was then that real fright caught up with her, sending ice-cold shivers along her spine, because Greg, her brother, and his wife, Annette, had been with her. She closed her eyes and saw them all fighting against the gale. She saw herself trying to open the hatch so that she could get whatever it was someone desperately wanted from below; wire clippers, 'Get the wire clippers ... get ... the ... wire clippers!' She couldn't move the hatch, and when she finally did, her lifeline was in the way. With the importance of the wire clippers uppermost in her mind, she undid the safety line for just one moment, and it was then the gigantic wave hit the yacht, sweeping her away with it as it receded. After that there was nothing but blackness. The starless sky had been as black as the water, and there was nothing else.

She had not lost consciousness. She began to swim instinctively, terrified of the great troughs and waves, but determined to survive. She wore a lifejacket, and it could only have been minutes before her hands came in contact with the lifebelt. Gasping, choking, beyond even the realms of fear, she had clung to it, letting it take her weight, and the motion of the water lifted and dropped her pitilessly until the black sky was tinted with the first grey streak of dawn and gradually changed through shades of pink to cloudy blue. By then she was drifting without being aware of anything except relief that the gale had eased and the sea was less angry. She didn't know that she was anywhere near land. It seemed as if there would never be anything else but sea and sky, and if she didn't keep repeating her name she would sink beneath the waves and be forgotten forever.

And now she was safe, lying on a hard, narrow bed in a quaint little room feeling weak and battered, but safe nevertheless. But where were the others? Had they not been so lucky? She wanted to ask the doctor, but couldn't form the words.

He saw her agitation and spoke to her soothingly in a foreign tongue. Then he called again to the man outside.

'Sam, you have a room, and the woman will take care of her. I have no women here. I will come and check on her daily and there will be no trouble. When she is rested she will be fine. She is strong.'

A shadow fell across the doorway. The other man was near. A new tenseness gripped her, constricting her heart so that she could hardly breathe.

'You can babble away as long as you like, my friend, but I won't be persuaded,' she heard him say. His voice was low-pitched and pleasantly slow, but quite decisive.

When he came into the tiny cubicle he was so big there hardly seemed room for anyone else. His head touched the rough ceiling, his shoulders were as wide as the doorway. The doctor moved to make space for him. He took a step towards the bed and Minella stared at him openly, the tenseness becoming a shield against vulnerability, because instinct warned her not to trust him. His shirt was now tucked firmly into a pair of tight, faded jeans, and he looked almost aggressive. His hair was dark, but lightened in places by the sun, and the neatly trimmed beard round his angular chin was threaded here and there with grey. The square face was bronzed and handsome with deep-set eyes beneath straight, dark brows, and the line of his mouth was firm and masterful.

'Sam, just for once will you listen to me . . .'

'Henrique, I've told you, I don't *want* the child in my house,' said Sam.

Minella summoned all her will-power and found strength to protest.

'Child!' she said, in the loudest voice she could manage. 'I'm *not* a child, and I can look after myself, thank you very much!'

He raised his eyebrows in surprise and a smile touched the stern mouth which had surely murmured gentler words earlier. She hadn't dreamt it.

'The little bird has talons, Henrique,' he said. Then he addressed her for the first time. 'Can you tell me your name?'

She frowned and tried so hard to remember that it brought fresh pain to her temples. How ridiculous! She shook her head slowly.

'No,' she said, sadly. 'I kept repeating it out loud when I was in the water, and now I've forgotten it.'

'Then I shall call you Sparrow,' said Sam. He turned to his friend. 'How about that?'

'Eh, what is that?' The fat man lifted his shoulders in perplexity.

'It is a little brown English bird. It suits her, don't you think, in spite of the sharp claws.'

'Ah, yes, yes.'

Her limbs felt as if they didn't belong to her, but she managed to extricate an arm from the blanket, and she touched her red-brown hair. It was dry now, but sticky with salt water and she knew she must look an awful mess. Her arm was bare. Someone had removed her sweat-shirt, and when she moved one foot against her leg she discovered that her jeans were missing, too. It dawned on her that she was probably naked under the blanket, and these two men must have been responsible for taking off her clothes. True, one was a doctor and used to such things, but the thought of the other one looking at her body made her burn with embarrassment. Her hand fell on to the pillow. She had never felt quite so weak.

His eyes were on her, his expression unfathomable. 'Don't worry, Sparrow,' he said. 'Dr Porva will look after you.'

He seemed influential. The doctor in no way intimidated him, and he was not going to be told what to do. The set of his head and his whole bearing were full of self-confidence.

'I'd prefer that,' said Minella. For some reason she felt a need to assert herself, to let him know she didn't want to be dependent on any begrudged hospitality even if he changed his mind.

He lifted her hand from the pillow, turning it in his.

Her nails had suffered while she was crewing and the skin of her palms was still crinkled from being in the water so long, but he held her hand gently, like something fragile, and seemed about to make quiet comment. Then, with a careless change of tactics, he dropped it back on the pillow.

'I'm going into town,' he said curtly. 'I'll let the Border Authorities in Horta know you're here. Perhaps they'll send someone to collect you as soon as you're able to travel.'

'Where *is* Horta?' she asked. 'Where am I?'

'Las Ilhas Atlânticas,' said Sam. 'The Azores to you.'

'And she is not fit to be moved as far as Horta for many hours yet,' said Henrique Porva, 'unless you arrange an ambulance. But you could take her to your house in a car.'

Sam's eyes blazed and it was easy to see he was not used to having his decisions questioned. 'I repeat, I am *not* taking charge of her. There are plenty of women in the village capable of it. If money's the problem, I'll pay someone.'

Minella propped herself up gingerly, anger now making her head spin.

'When you've finished discussing me as if I'm a bit of flotsam you found washed up perhaps *I* can have a say in the matter!' she cried. 'I *want* to go to Horta, if that's where I can find out who I am, and what's happened to the people who were with me.'

'I shall try to find out for you,' said Sam. '*You* will stay here.'

And he strode away, ducking his head under a low beam as he left the tiny room. A bang reverberated through the whole building when he slammed the main door.

'Well!' gasped Minella, lying back with relief.

'Ah, he is a difficult man,' said Dr Porva, gesticulating with his hands. But there was a canny twinkle in his eyes which meant the reproof was not to be taken too seriously. There was obviously a strong bond between the two men. 'Today I will see my patients and not ask them to lie down. If anyone needs to lie down they must come again tomorrow. Today they will *all* come here, but only because they know I have a beautiful young girl in my surgery who was rescued from the sea. Curiosity . . . is that what you call it? But I shall tell them you are sleeping. You will sleep now, won't you, Spar—ho.'

She smiled for the first time. 'Sparrow,' she corrected.

'You are a brave girl,' he said, and leaned over to pat her arm.

He went away, and came back a short time later with something rather like porridge in a dish, and helped her to eat it. Surprisingly she managed it, and even found it tasted good.

She tried not to think about the storm that had come up with hardly any warning, the violent gale that had driven them off course, but it kept coming back to her. A vague, unpleasant ache brought a frown to her forehead as fragments of conversation she had heard refused to make sense, and she found it hard to distinguish between dreams and reality. Dr Porva had talked about more survivors, but that must be because he thought she had come from a shipwreck. He didn't know she had been washed overboard and was the only one missing from a crew of six. Everyone else would be all right. But what had they done when they found out what had happened? Had they tried to turn back, facing into the terrible wind to search for her, and were they searching still? Or had they abandoned hope of finding her and carried on? Her brother would be frantic with grief.

She started trying to tell the doctor what had happened, but it was too complicated just then, and she only managed the one elusive fact that meant so much to her.

'Dr Porva, I've remembered my name. It's Minella Farmer.'

'That is very pretty,' he said. He busied himself with bottles in a cabinet on the wall, shook two tablets into his hand, then fetched a glass of water from the other room. 'Now, I am going to give you something to make you sleep, and when you wake up you will feel rested. Then you can tell me all about yourself.'

She swallowed the tablets and lay down again when he touched her shoulder authoritatively.

'Why doesn't the man called Sam want me at his house?' she asked. 'Tell me about him.'

Henrique Porva shrugged. 'Sam Stafford is a very good friend, but he has some . . . hang-upwards.'

'Hang-ups,' giggled Minella, loving his attempt at colloquial English.

'Yes. I do not think he likes women.'

'Oh.' There was so much she wanted to ask this kind Azorean doctor, but she was very drowsy. 'Why doesn't he like them?'

If he answered she didn't hear him. Her limbs felt deliciously relaxed and she closed her eyes. She would have to ask him again later.

When she awoke again there was a woman speaking excitedly in Portuguese to Dr Porva. Minella, fascinated, wished she could understand them. After a while the woman came into the room, a bright smile lighting her face when she saw that Minella was awake. She wore a coloured, peasant-type skirt with a black blouse, and a cotton scarf covered her black hair. It was difficult to guess her age, but her figure was ample, to say the least, and a tracery of lines creased the skin at the corners of her eyes.

'O senhora, we are come to take you somewhere more comfortable,' she said. 'How are you?'

'I feel fine now,' said Minella, and sat up quickly, swinging her legs off the bed without thinking. To her relief she saw that she was still wearing her bra and pants, but then the room started spinning round again and she fell back on the pillow with a little groan of frustration.

The woman clucked like a worried hen. 'There, there, you are still very weak. Do not worry, I will get Vasco to carry you. It is why I brought him. Vasco is my nephew. I am Benita.'

Dr Porva came into the room behind her, full of apologies.

'I am so sorry, I cannot keep you here. I was on the telephone to Benita because she is a good woman and will look after you.' He came and put a hand on her forehead, then took her pulse, and the twinkle was back in his eyes. 'I must take this first, young lady, before you see Vasco. He is a very handsome boy, and I have told him you are a beautiful girl. He cannot wait to see you.'

'We will put these on,' said Benita. She was holding Minella's jeans and sweat-shirt which had been rough-dried. They were hard and uncomfortable, but she felt happier with them on, especially when Benita signalled for her nephew to come in.

The tiny room was overcrowded, yet she could breathe more easily than when Sam had been standing there. His aversion had created an atmosphere and his size had been intimidating. But Vasco was different. Minella had a knack of making good spot judgments, and decided at once that he would be a friend she could trust. He looked to be about her own age and had real Latin charm; black hair, a lithe, sinewy body, and shining black eyes which lighted on her with equal appreciation.

'The doctor, he was right,' said Vasco, smiling warmly.

'Hello,' said Minella.

Dr Porva was still full of apologies while he made sure the blanket was securely wrapped round her.

'I wish I could take you to Benita's myself, but already I am late with my visits, so I have a taxi waiting. Vasco will take you out to it.'

'But I can walk,' Minella protested.

'And disappoint him? No, it is better not.'

She held out her hands to the doctor and thanked him for all he had done, then once again she was picked up in masculine arms, only this time it was not the same. Vasco was not so tall or so broad as Sam, and he was clumsy.

'Be careful with her,' Benita warned, as he carried her out into the sunshine.

'I shall see you again,' said Henrique Porva, and the words were comforting, because Minella had a momentary feeling of unease once she left the security of the four walls. She had recollections of bandits on foreign islands who abducted people and held them to ransom. Not that it would be worth the trouble where she was concerned, but she was at their mercy and she wished, illogically, that the Englishman hadn't disappeared quite so quickly.

She looked around and saw that she was in a fishing village where low stone walls climbed gradually upwards from a bay, and square cottages were only a stone's throw from the whaleboats pulled up on the beach. There was an air of tranquillity about the place, as if time stood still.

The taxi was an old, bulbous Chevrolet. Vasco deposited her on the back seat while the driver held open the door, and they talked together in their peculiar Portuguese which could almost have been mistaken for French. She smiled, knowing they were talking about her, and when Benita settled her bulk in the seat beside her, giving the car a decided tilt to one side, it was hard to keep a straight face.

The taxi revved and coughed, and started an uncomfortable journey out of the village along a lonely road where other motor transport seemed to be non-existent. But the jolting was soon forgotten. Minella had never seen such colourful landscape, or realised there were so many shades of green, and she gazed out of the window in wonder. A patchwork of fields, richly green and yellow and blue, was stitched together with low rocky walls, and meadows were edged unbelievably with beautiful blue hydrangeas. The road was narrow and winding, and round one corner they had to pull up sharply to make room for an ox-cart with high wicker sides, a harvest of straw piled so high it looked top-heavy. The wooden wheels with their sawmill screech made her cover her ears until the load was out of sight.

Benita didn't speak, but Vasco turned now and then to smile at Minella, as if making sure she was still there. Her face was bathed in perspiration and she unravelled herself from the blanket, feeling suffocated and anything but attractive. It was surprising he looked at her at all.

A bit further on, Benita leaned forward and gave instructions to the driver. He turned off the road and on to an even narrower track, which didn't please Vasco at all. He began to quarrel with Benita. Their voices rose, as deafening as the ox-cart wheels, but they probably sounded angrier than they were because she didn't understand the language. Minella shrank into the corner of the car. When it stopped a few minutes later she was greatly relieved, and half afraid to look out of the window. But when she saw the view everything else was forgotten.

They had arrived at a low cottage with a rust-red tiled roof and whitewashed walls, much like others she had seen, but bits had been added to make the shape irregular, and one wall was covered with vines. The garden was overflowing with azaleas and flaming canna lilies. Below it, at what must have been the bottom of a steep drop, was a lake, the water as clear as blue stained glass, and on the far side sheer cliffs climbed up towards the sky.

'Oh, it's so beautiful,' Minella breathed. 'Who lives here?'

'I do,' said Benita.

Vasco was still angry for some reason and he jumped

out of the car, slamming the door. But when he looked at Minella his expression softened and he gestured with his hands, his shoulders lifting with resignation.

'I am not happy to leave you here,' he said, 'but I will carry you in, and then I must return to work.'

She tossed the blanket aside and tested her legs. 'I think I'd rather walk,' she said.

She was beginning to feel like a parcel being dumped first one place, then another, and she made a determined effort to climb out of the car and stand on the uneven path.

'As you wish,' said Vasco, a little stiffly. 'I shall come to see you as soon as I think it is . . . convenient. Goodbye.'

Benita addressed him rapidly in Portuguese and he glanced at the cottage with a belligerent shake of his head before making off at an angle from the road. Benita sighed, gave the taxi driver some money, and turned to Minella.

'He is a strange boy sometimes,' she said. 'I do not understand him.'

Minella thought so, too, but the sun was beating down on her head and her eyes didn't feel up to coping with the glare much longer, so she took a few tentative steps and was glad to find her legs returning to normal. It was a relief to reach the door.

Inside it was cool. A fan revolved in the ceiling, and plain wooden furniture had an uncluttered look on the tiled floor where bright tapestry rugs were scattered. The roof extended out like a canopy from the main room, keeping out the sun and forming a patio with a glorious view of the lake. Somehow she wouldn't have expected Benita to live in such a place.

'Now,' she said, making Minella sit in the most comfortable chair, 'I will make coffee, and then you go to bed. Tomorrow you will be better, yes?'

'Yes,' said Minella, very definitely. 'And I don't want to go to bed.'

Benita planted her feet in the middle of one of the rugs and put her hands on her hips. 'The doctor Henrique, he says you are to sleep today, and I must see that you do. Soon I will take you to the bedroom.'

Alone for several minutes, Minella looked round uneasily. She felt on edge. There was something wrong somewhere, but she couldn't put her finger on what it was. Too tidy, perhaps. She felt it even more when she went into the bedroom, yet it was a light, attractive room overlooking the garden and had a fan to cool the air. The roughcast walls were dramatically white, but a lavishly embroidered cover on the bed softened the starkness otherwise relieved only by plain burnt-orange curtains. On the wall opposite the bed there was a painting of a weird construction that looked like a cross between a scarecrow and a bunch of bananas which she studied for a moment, then blinked and turned away. It was not the type of room Benita would use. She was sure of that, even on such short acquaintance. There was a well-ordered atmosphere about it that repelled her slightly, and she wondered whether she would have still felt the same if Vasco hadn't behaved so oddly when the taxi brought them here.

'I have brought you my nightgown,' Benita was saying. 'I will take your clothes and wash them while you sleep, yes?'

'Thank you,' said Minella. She wouldn't have dared to disobey. 'But could I wash first, please? I seem to smell of salt water.'

'Of course, of course.'

A warm bath did more than anything to restore her morale, though Benita wouldn't allow her to linger in it. The nightdress was a sleeveless, voluminous cotton which would have fitted two as diminutive as Minella, but it smelled as fresh as the summer air, and the feel of it against her skin was soothing after the salt-caked underwear she had discarded. The sheets on the bed were equally welcoming and she had to admit that all she wanted to do was lie between them and let the rest of the world take care of itself for a little while longer. In no time at all she was sleeping like a baby.

It was not really a sound that woke her. She had come to the surface of sleep where consciousness is only a breath away, and she was vaguely aware that someone different had come into the room. She could feel a pair of eyes gazing upon her with more than casual concern, boring into her, disturbing her greatly even before she was properly awake. Without daring to look she knew exactly who was standing over her, and her heart lurched.

'Who the hell brought you here when I absolutely forbade it?' came the furious demand.

It was the Englishman, Sam Stafford.

CHAPTER TWO

MINELLA sat up in the bed, clutching the sheet firmly beneath her chin because Benita's nightdress wouldn't stay on her shoulders. There wasn't a sound in the house except for the quiet whirring of the fan above which ruffled her red-brown hair and made it flick over her forehead. Her brown eyes were wide with amazement and she licked her lips.

'I'm sorry—Benita said she lived here.'

'She does, but she isn't here now,' said Sam, his voice clipped with disapproval. 'I've been out all day and I came back expecting a meal to be ready. Just wait till I get my hands on that woman!'

His anger sent a shiver of apprehension through Minella.

'Is she your wife?' she ventured to ask. She couldn't picture him married to anyone of Benita's proportions, but you never could tell. Why would he be living on a remote island if it wasn't because he was married to one of the inhabitants?

'No, she is *not* my wife,' he said adamantly. 'I don't have a wife. Never have had, and never will.'

Minella was blessed with a quick sense of humour which sometimes got her into trouble, and it caught up with her now so that she had to pull the sheet up even higher to hide the smile that threatened to turn into a giggle.

'What a rash statement!' she said. 'It doesn't sound to me as if anyone would want you anyway.'

She ought not to have spoken like that to someone she had only just met, but she couldn't help it. His arrogance surprised her, but certainly didn't impress her, and she made up her mind not to stay a moment

22

longer than necessary where she wasn't welcome. She would leave at the first opportunity.

But he was giving the matter thought, and something that resembled an answering smile hovered at the corners of his lips.

'You could be right at that,' he agreed. 'The trouble is I've lived alone too long. Benita is my housekeeper. She has her own quarters at the back of the house.' He paused, and looked at her critically. 'The important thing now, though, is what are we going to do about you?'

'I'm better,' said Minella. 'If you like *I'll* cook you a meal. I'm quite a good cook.'

'You will do no such thing!' The colour which had returned to her cheeks after resting ebbed away when she made a hurried move to get up. 'You will stay where you are and behave yourself, then if you're stronger tomorrow we'll see what other arrangements can be made. I hope you're not worried about your reputation.'

'Why should I be?'

The light was fading quickly and she realised it was evening already. The day had passed unnoticed except for the short periods of wakefulness that had been like cameos set apart from time. Sam Stafford lit a lamp beside the bed which cast shadows.

'It looks like you'll be spending the night alone with me. Benita won't come back now—she doesn't like the dark.' He stood up straight and ran his fingers through his hair. 'Wretched woman!'

'You mustn't talk about her like that,' Minella protested. 'She was very kind to me.'

'Of course she was. It would amuse her greatly to dump a young girl in my bed and then run off rather than face me.'

'*Your* bed!'

'That's right. It's only a small cottage.'

Minella wriggled her toes, feeling vastly uncomfortable at the discovery, but there was nothing she could do to alter the situation. If anyone had told her a few days ago that she would find herself in an isolated cottage, alone with a man she didn't know, she would have been horrified, but it had happened, and somehow she wasn't frightened.

All the same, it gave her a peculiar prickly feeling to know she was occupying the bed in which he normally slept.

'Where will *you* spend the night?' she asked, with only a faint tremor in her voice.

His smile was cynical. 'There's a sun-bed on the patio. But don't worry, I'm kind to children and animals and I've never attacked anybody yet.'

He turned to leave, and as he did so Minella picked up a hairbrush from the bedside table and threw it at him, missing his head by a fraction of an inch.

'I'm *not* a child!' she yelled, 'So please don't treat me like one!'

He stopped. His back was as straight as a knife, the atmosphere as sharp, and when he looked at her sparks were flying. She didn't know what madness had prompted her to do such a silly thing. His words hadn't really merited it, but it was the insult behind them that had infuriated her, as if she was not worth bothering about.

'Then don't ever do such a childish thing again.' He bent down and retrieved the brush, tapping the bristles against his palm. 'If you weren't convalescing I'd have no compunction about putting you across my knee and tanning your backside with it!'

She was not subdued. His reaction made her tingle and she would have relished a fight, but she was a guest in his house, albeit an unwanted one, and it would have been impolite.

'I'm sorry,' she apologised. 'I didn't intend to hit you with it, but I hate being spoken to as if I'm about fourteen.'

He sat on the edge of the bed, weighing her up thoroughly with smoky blue eyes before saying anything else. Then: 'Would you prefer me to treat you like the woman you very obviously are?'

His gaze had dropped downwards from her face and she was suddenly aware that when she had thrown the brush the sheet had slipped, and so had Benita's nightdress, leaving one shoulder bare and her breasts clearly visible through the flimsy material. She gasped and slid hurriedly down the bed until only those big brown eyes showed above the sheet.

He laughed, a loud, warm, humorous laugh that filled the room. Then he leaned over and put his hands on the bed each side of her body, pinioning her down. Her heart began to race. He was near enough for her to see a pulse throbbing in his throat, and a mat of brown hair curled at the open neck of his shirt. His lips curved into a smile which caused singing in her ears and she was so hot it seemed the ceiling fan must have been switched off, but she couldn't move. She had never felt such feverish excitement leap in her body before, and if he had bent his head further and kissed her, as she feared he might do, she would have responded to him without a doubt. He was hypnotising her.

'No,' she murmured, in answer to a question asked an age ago and lost somewhere amidst a host of unspoken questions which went much deeper. 'I'd just like to be left alone, please.'

She couldn't begin to analyse the way she felt. Powerful physical attraction such as this was new to her, and she felt vaguely ashamed. Sam Stafford must never know what havoc he had created in these moments of weakness. Tomorrow he wouldn't have this awful effect on her.

'How old are you, Sparrow?' he asked.

'Twenty.'

He eased himself back, allowing her to breathe again.

'And I'm thirty-five, so you see to me you're still very young.'

'Such a great age,' she murmured, with suitable awe, and the relief at being released from his sorcery was so great she grinned. 'By the way, my name is Minella.'

'Minella. That's pretty.' With his index finger he traced a line from the dimple in her cheek to the tip of her chin, and she quivered. 'But I shall still call you Sparrow.'

'Not for long. Tomorrow you can have your bed back.'

'I intend to. I shall take you back to Henrique and he can find other lodgings for you until arrangements can be made for you to fly home. Meanwhile you'll have to put up with my cooking.'

He left her sitting up in bed, a protest on her lips which she knew it was no use voicing. There was a lot she wanted to ask him. Whether he had heard any news of the race and the yachts caught up in the storm. Whether there had been any radio contact, or enquiries about her. She would have to wait until later, but impatience made her restless and she fidgeted with the pillow and crumpled the sheet until she could bear it no longer. Putting her feet to the ground with care, she stood up experimentally and finding herself quite steady she wound the sheet round her like a sarong before padding out in search of the kitchen.

'Mr Stafford, I'm sorry, but I can't stay in bed. I never could, even when I was little.'

'And you're not much bigger now.' He turned half round, as if he had been expecting her. A large butcher's apron covered the front of him and a delicious smell of cooking wafted through the house. She was very hungry. 'You'd better call me Sam. No one knows me by any other name round here. And if you're staying up for dinner put some clothes on. You'll put me off eating.'

'I haven't got any clothes,' she said angrily. 'Benita took them away to wash.'

He stirred the contents of a cooking pot on the stove and tasted a little on the tip of a spoon like every good chef.

'Go back to the bedroom, then,' he commanded.

'I'm not going to eat my dinner in bed!'

'If you argue any more you won't get any. Now be a good girl and do as I say. In a minute I'll bring you something to wear.'

He was impossible! A bit of civility would go a long way and she wanted to tell him so, but there was no point in starting a slanging match, and the food smelled much too good to risk missing. Her legs felt wobbly again and she held on to the wall as she went back along the passage that separated the kitchen from the rest of the house. Why was Sam so impatient with her? He could at least make an effort to be pleasant, even if she had been foisted on him unexpectedly. It wasn't as if she was likely to make a habit of dropping in for the evening.

She sat on the bed and waited, and presently he came in. There was a large chest of drawers at one end of the room and he went to it and pulled open one of the drawers. She could see his things were neatly folded and he drew out a pair of white jeans and a blue shirt, tossing them over to her.

'Put those on,' he said.

She caught them, almost overbalancing, and it was her turn to protest.

'I can't wear these—they're yours. Isn't there something of Benita's I could use?'

'I don't go into Benita's room, and judging by the sight of you in one of her nightgowns I doubt whether any of her other clothes would be an improvement. You'll have to make do.' He shut the drawer and ducked his head under the doorway as he left. 'When you're ready, go out on the patio. We'll eat out there, it's cooler.'

Minella held the pants and shirt with reluctance.

They had been washed many times and creases which regularly appeared when the material was moulded to his body had become immune to the iron. She didn't want to put them on. There was something too personal about the touch of them against her skin, and it took a little while to overcome the automatic rejection. But she had to wear something or she wouldn't be getting any dinner, so she had no choice.

Sam had narrow hips. The jeans were not too bad a fit round her waist and when the legs had been rolled up half a dozen times they were fairly presentable. The shirt was a different matter. It fell off her shoulders much as the nightie had done, and she found the only way she could keep it on was to knot it firmly across the front. Then she picked up the brush and drew it through her hair, wishing it could have been shampooed. Sam's impression of her wasn't going to improve much when he saw this urchin, but it couldn't be helped. It would have been nice if she'd been able to make an entrance on to the patio looking a picture of sophistication even in borrowed gear, then his expression might have registered something other than mere tolerance. But you had to be tall to look good in just any old thing, and Minella hadn't a hope.

When he saw her he smiled. The steaming bowls of soup in either hand were set down on the table while he studied her, whether with amusement or approval she couldn't tell. It made her uncomfortable, and she slipped quickly into the chair he indicated.

The soup was delicious, and she guessed it was made with fresh vegetables, but she would have enjoyed it more if she hadn't been aware of Sam's continued scrutiny. She savoured each spoonful, afraid to look up because she knew if she did she would meet his eyes. It was unnerving and showed a lack of manners that aggravated her so much she put down her spoon and met his gaze full on. Damn the man, he was enjoying her discomfort!

'I haven't taken a vow of silence,' she said. 'Have you? You haven't spoken a word since we sat down.'

'This isn't a smart restaurant requiring smart conversation.' He pushed aside his dish. 'I'm sorry, Sparrow, I'm not used to entertaining.'

A lamp on the table attracted moths and she watched them flutter helplessly against the glass. Why should she feel equally helpless in the presence of this enigmatic stranger? He was treating her well and she wasn't afraid of him, yet she had the feeling he would rebuff any real overture of friendship. Was it possible that he was the one who was embarrassed at having a girl here in his house all night.

'Is it me you don't like, or people in general?' she asked. 'You've really shut yourself away from civilisation, haven't you?'

'It's the way I like it,' he said. 'And how could I possibly dislike a little thing like you.' His hand covered hers in a brief gesture of reassurance, but she drew it away immediately. 'Except when you throw things at me.'

Her cheeks coloured and she looked down at her hands, fingering the place where his hand touched as if trying to erase the warm sensation caused by the contact. She didn't know whether she liked him or not, but physically she would never be indifferent to him, and she saw danger where before there had seemed to be none. There was an undercurrent between them which couldn't be explained, and which she certainly couldn't deny. Perhaps she was just being over-sensitive, letting her imagination run away with her, but it served as a warning.

'Tomorrow,' she said, 'I've got to find out whether my brother and sister-in-law have been in touch with anyone. I must let them know I'm safe. We were all taking part in a yacht race, but I was swept overboard in the storm.'

'I know,' said Sam. 'I've been making enquiries for you.'

'Oh!' Her eyes were anxious. 'Please tell me what you found out.'

'Very little, I'm afraid. The authorities in Bermuda lost radio contact with most of the yachts owing to weather conditions, but they're gradually being accounted for. I've asked for any new information to be phoned through to me.'

'Thank you. But how did you know anything about me when I couldn't even tell you my name?'

He gathered the soup bowls together and stood up.

'It wasn't too difficult,' he said. 'I'm interested in ocean racing and the Westerly Cup always attracts a lot of entries. I've been following it, so I knew some of the yachts would be in the vicinity if the gale blew them off course. Then you very sensibly had a lifebelt from the boat round you, which spoke for itself.'

He went back to the kitchen and she felt as if she had been put in her place. He obviously thought she was a bit of an idiot.

The main meal consisted of smoked sausage and pork cooked with peas and tomatoes, which he told her was a favourite Azorean dish. She was getting tired again and much as she had fancied solid food she found herself unable to cope with so much. Afraid of offending him, she ate what she could, but had to give up after a few mouthfuls.

'You don't have to eat it, Sparrow,' he said kindly. 'It's probably all wrong for an invalid anyway.'

'It tastes so good and I hate to leave it. Normally I'd scoff the lot.'

He smiled. 'Don't worry, Benita will take what's left tomorrow for that no-good nephew of hers.'

'Do you mean Vasco?' she asked in surprise.

'I do mean Vasco. How come you know him?' Sam was scowling now, peering at her from beneath lowered brows.

'He carried me from Dr Porva's house to the taxi. Benita told me who he was.'

'Hmmm,' he growled. 'Just see he doesn't get as close to you again.'

'He's not likely to when I'm leaving first thing in the morning,' said Minella.

She objected to him giving her orders, and closed her eyes, hoping that was the end of the matter because she hadn't strength to argue with him. Seeing her fatigue, he came round and opened the sun-bed.

'Lie down,' he commanded.

That did it. 'Don't speak to me as if I'm a pet dog!' she shouted. 'I know I'm a nuisance, but I didn't ask to come here!'

Sam paused a moment, taken aback by her retaliation. Then he came up behind her and put his hands on her shoulders. 'I ought to have forbidden you to leave that bed. If Henrique knew you were up and dressed he'd slay me, but I feel as if I'm up against a wild thing. Whatever I say you let fly at me. Are you as wilful as this at home?'

Minella didn't answer. He was massaging her shoulders and the gentle pressure of his thumbs at the nape of her neck sent exquisite waves of pleasure through her body, making her incapable of uttering any sound except a slow, gasping breath. She arched her back and stretched her neck luxuriously, then shrugged him away, because such sensuality was too potent by far and the language of his hands frightened her.

'I'm on edge,' she said. 'I can't seem to cope with someone like you right now. I'm sorry.'

She went over to the sun-bed and found it was a relief to lie down again. She had never been ill in her life and was cross with herself for being so weak, but willpower was not enough to overcome it. Sam stood over her, his expression too complicated to read.

'I'm sorry, too,' he said. 'I ought to have more patience. It's what comes of always living alone.'

He turned and left her, disappearing into the house, and the careless apology hung there where it had been delivered. She didn't know what to think. She didn't like him, but he intrigued her, and she was dying to know why he lived here as he did. He was a sort of exile, though whether by choice or force of circumstances she had yet to discover. He was certainly not the man to welcome an invasion of his privacy, so she didn't know how she was going to manage it, and as she was not going to be with him for much longer she probably never would. How maddening!

The moon was coming up and the lake shone like darkened glass now, the cliffs on the far side looming gaunt and forbidding against the night sky, but the garden hummed with nocturnal insects and a fragrance of flowers filled the air. It was an idyllic place. Yet Minella was conscious of some great disturbance below the surface, something that had existed in the past. Sam Stafford and his island were strangely similar.

He was taking up too many of her thoughts. Her main worry was about Greg and Annette. She closed her eyes, trying to shut out the haunting beauty of her surroundings, because by now they would have given her up for lost.

When Greg's friend had asked for her to be included in the crew of the yacht she had been thrilled and excited, knowing it to be a big tribute to her sailing skill, but Greg had tried to forbid it. Although Minella was expert with small craft, she had not had enough experience to take part in a long-distance race, particularly one as gruelling as the Westerly Cup, and he had argued that she was not ready for it. But Minella had a way of getting what she wanted. It was a chance she had been longing for, and nothing was going to stop her. After all, if Annette was considered good enough to crew, it would have been quite unfair to take one and not the other, because there was no denying that Minella was better at handling boats than her sister-in-law. But Annette had had holiday experience on board the ten-ton yacht, and was a tall, strong girl, whereas Minella's diminutive size was another disadvantage. Greg stuck out until the last minute, but then someone had dropped out, and he had given way to his sister.

When the storm struck it had been all hands on deck, the men wrestling with the sails. Hammered by heavy seas and stinging rain driving against her face, Minella had worked as hard as the rest, and nobody had thought it necessary to keep an eye on her. The west wind which was supposed to blow across the Atlantic had changed to a violent easterly gale, gathering force every second, and as they drove into the face of it she almost wished she had listened to her brother. She was terrified, yet exhilarated at the same time. In the pitch black night, with the fury of the gale and the sea roaring in everyone's ears, her screams must have gone unheard, and it had probably been quite a while before they missed her.

Poor Greg! She couldn't bear to think how he must be feeling.

There was a step outside in the garden. Stealthy feet rustled the grass, hardly audible, but Minella was in a highly sensitive state and the sound reached her more as an intuition than a certainty.

She stayed motionless, not knowing whether to shout for Sam, or remain undetected until the prowler went away. Her heartbeats quickened. Why would anyone want to creep up on this remote cottage? The footsteps came nearer and she held her breath, goose pimples coming up on her arms. Whoever it was didn't want to be seen, and neither did Minella. She was glad the sun-bed was at the side of the patio and not in full view of anyone approaching. A figure appeared, dimly at first, moving slowly into the open. Then he was silhouetted against the sky as he surveyed the patio and accustomed his eyes to the light. He saw Minella, and came forward.

'I was hoping you would be here,' he said, in a sort of stage whisper.

If he had sprung at her gangster fashion it couldn't have surprised her more than hearing herself addressed by someone who knew her. He didn't come full into the light immediately, and it took several seconds for her to recognise the intruder. When she did, she laughed.

'Vasco! Why are you creeping about as if you're afraid of being seen? Sam's indoors. Shall I call him?'

'No, no, no.' Vasco crouched down beside her sunbed, keeping his head low and his voice even lower. 'He doesn't like me coming here, but Benita sent me with a message. I give it to you instead and you can tell him.'

'But why?' Minella was puzzled. He was such a nice boy, and surely the nephew of his housekeeper would be welcome in Sam Stafford's house. It was taking the solitude business a bit far if he excluded everyone. She had never come across a genuine hermit before, but Sam was beginning to fit the description. '*I'm* pleased you've come, and I'm sure Sam won't really mind.'

Vasco put a finger to his lips. 'He is a strange man with things to hide. I think he is afraid of people asking questions. I wish Benita had brought you to our house, but there is no room. We have my grandfather sick.'

'Oh, I'm sorry. I hope it isn't serious.'

'He is an old man with a heart that goes boom-boom.' He put his hand to his chest dramatically, but then a grin spread across his face and though the pitch of his voice remained the same, the timbre changed. 'And I am a young man whose heart goes boom-boom when I look at you. I would care for you very well at our house, *o senhora*. I do not like you being alone with . . . him.' A jerk of his head in the direction of the door indicated that he meant Sam.

The black wavy hair on a level with her nose smelled strongly of perfume, and his handsome features were etched in bold lines and shaded by the lamplight. Black eyes glittered. She would be about as safe with Vasco as she had been clinging to her lifebelt all night.

'Tell me, why doesn't he like questions?' Minella

asked, partly to change the subject, and partly because her curiosity was aroused and she wanted to hear everything he knew about Sam Stafford. The man was becoming more intriguing by the hour. She, too, spoke in a whisper, as if it was a conspiracy.

'There is not time now. I will tell you things tomorrow, or the next day, when he is not here.' He let his eyes dwell on her, and their message was clear.

'But I'm leaving in the morning.'

He was desolate. 'You cannot do that! I must get to know you first. I do not even know your name and already I think I am in love. I will die if you go away so soon.'

Minella burst out laughing. She'd heard of Latin lovers working fast and being outrageous flirts, but this was ridiculous. She would have to be careful not to give him the slightest encouragement. Yet she couldn't help liking him.

'Sam calls me Sparrow,' she said.

'And that is your name?'

'No. It's just what he calls me.'

'Then I will not use that word the same as him.' Indignation made his voice rise, and he was leaning closer. Minella flattened herself back against the cushion, wishing he would stand up and behave normally. At home she could handle infatuated boyfriends, and there had been one or two, but this gorgeous, impetuous young man was an unknown quantity. If she rebuffed him he might become even more temperamental, but she couldn't allow this charade to continue.

She was on the point of calling for Sam as a last resort when a single word was spoken behind them, cutting as a whiplash.

'Vasco!' Sam was standing in the doorway, legs astride, anger apparent in every inch of him. 'Get away from Minella! And haven't I told you before not to come here.'

Vasco stumbled to his feet, but he was not intimidated. His eyes glittered even more and she could tell they were old antagonists.

'I come because Benita sent me,' he said. 'Never would I come here otherwise. Never!' He spat on the ground to demonstrate his aversion. 'She wished me to tell you that her father, my grandfather, is ill and she cannot leave him.'

'Thank you. Is that all?' The sarcasm was so heavy in Sam's tone it made Minella jumpy. Whatever was the matter with the two of them? Surely Sam was old enough to know better.

'No,' said Vasco. 'I do not like the *senhora* staying with you. I wish to take her to my aunt's house.'

'You won't take Minella anywhere, now or ever. I didn't choose to have her as a guest, but she's here and it's where she'll stay.'

'I do not trust you.'

'Trust! *You* talk about trust!' He took a threatening step towards the younger man. 'I don't know why I'm even bothering to talk to you. Get out!'

Minella stood up, her legs so shaky it could only be nerves that were making them worse.

'Will you both stop it!' she cried. 'Whatever grievances you have against each other, please don't use *me* to aggravate them. I would rather go back to Dr Porva's and spend the night in his surgery. Anything would be better than this.'

Vasco was contrite. '*O senhora*, I am sorry. It is just that I shall worry about you, you understand.'

'Thank you,' said Minella, sincerely. 'Now perhaps it would be wise if you leave.'

'For you I will do anything.' He took her hand and lifted it to his lips, and if the tension had not been so great she would have wanted to laugh. No one had ever treated her with such gallantry.

'Don't touch her!' Sam snapped.

Vasco slowly backed away, an insolent smile on his

face. 'Until we meet again,' he said, and disappeared swiftly into the shadows.

The silence after he had gone could have been cut with a knife. Sam's bad temper simmered and he glared at her as if it was all her fault.

'You were very rude to him,' she ventured, unable to stand the silence any longer.

'That boy is trouble,' said Sam. 'Keep away from him.'

The order was issued so abruptly and with such slighting coldness that Minella's own patience evaporated and she turned on him.

'Why should I?' she demanded. 'How do I know you are any better than he is? I've only just met the pair of you, and I'm beginning to wish I hadn't. What sort of place is this? A desert island where the arrival of a woman is so extraordinary all the men start tearing each other to pieces. It's ridiculous!'

His shoulder muscles slackened and he permitted a smile to ease the tightness of his mouth, though it didn't reach his eyes.

'Don't kid yourself, Sparrow. There are far more important things to think about than women. Believe me, I know.'

Somewhere in the house the phone started ringing. It had an antiquated sound quite different from the telephone at home, but its insistence was the same. He ignored it for a moment, still considering the issue he had raised, and she felt there was more behind the words than she would ever know. Then he went inside and the bell stopped ringing.

She wanted to go back to bed, but hadn't the strength to put one foot before the other, so she stood where she was, staring out at the lake. The moon climbed higher and silvered the garden and the water beyond it. It seemed as if another storm had passed.

Minella could hear the murmur of his voice in the distance, but it dropped so low she couldn't distinguish it from the dreamy sounds all around. Sam Stafford had been hurt in the past—hurt badly. That must be why he lived in seclusion and hated visitors, particularly females. Unless he had something to hide, and that was more than likely from the hints that Vasco had let slip.

Supposing he was a criminal gone to ground here, safe from British law? There were plenty who had left England and vanished without trace. If so, of what crime was he guilty, and how safe was she here alone with him, miles from any form of help?

Until now she had had no doubts about his integrity. He spoke her language and he had carried her up from the sea in strong, dependable arms which had lulled her into a feeling of security. She had had confidence in him. But now she was uneasy and wished Vasco hadn't come with his plausible insinuations, or at least not until the morning. Daylight always made night-time fears lose some of their credibility. And it was as well to be forewarned that there could be danger.

Her body was tense as she listened for him to come back to the patio. What greater danger could there be than the terrifying experience she had lived through last night? After that, surely there was no need for her to be afraid. All the same, she held her breath as a soft tread announced his approach.

He came and stood behind her, so close she could feel the warmth of his body against her, and when she would have turned to face him he prevented it with firm hands clamped on her shoulders. When he spoke his face was against her hair and his voice was gentle.

'Sparrow, I'm afraid it's bad news.' He paused a second, trying to ease the shock that was to come. 'The yacht you were on didn't make it through the storm. Wreckage has been identified, and there were no survivors. I can't tell you how sorry I am.'

Minella tried to speak, but instead she slipped from his grasp and began a long journey through darkness as she collapsed on the floor.

CHAPTER THREE

A STRONG wind was blowing and the sound of the sea was roaring in her ears. She was cold; so cold. She really ought to have worn her sheepskin coat, because it was always like this when an east wind swept along the coast and set the small craft bobbing in the marina. Silly to be walking along Brighton seafront in only a T-shirt and jeans on a day like this. Silly.

Minella tossed on the bed and her teeth were chattering. Someone switched off the ceiling fan and brought another blanket, wrapping it firmly round her. She didn't know where she was. One minute it seemed she was at home in England and the next she was on an island, and both places were deserted except for herself. Where had everyone gone? She called out for her brother Greg.

'It's all right, Sparrow,' a calm, consoling voice soothed her, and a hand stroked the hair away from her damp forehead. 'You'll soon feel better, little one.'

She looked up at him and his eyes were full of concern. He sponged her face and neck and hands, his touch so gentle she felt happy and loved.

'Hold me, Greg,' she whispered.

Her brother was ten years her senior and even when she was a child he had looked after her. She loved him dearly. Their father had died very suddenly of a coronary when she was still a baby and she couldn't remember him, so Greg had become the man of the family, almost a father figure to the small girl, although he was so young. She had grown up knowing he was the one she could turn to no matter what the problem. Greg was always there when she needed him, and she needed him now.

'Please hold me, Greg,' she insisted again.

Strong arms gathered her up and she was cradled against a broad chest that was warm and familiar. Her cheek lay on a linen shirt and the hand supporting her head pressed her closer. She heard him murmur something, but the words were lost because his mouth was against her hair and she was too drowsy to tell him she couldn't hear. There was some sort of hammering going on, loud, rhythmic thudding in her ear, and only when it continued incessantly did she realise it was his heart. Why should Greg's heart beat so fast? Perhaps he'd come running to find her. She stretched up her hand to his face, wanting to tell him how glad she was he had come, and her fingers encountered a bearded chin. Greg had never grown a beard.

She cried out.

Now she was hot. Her body was on fire and she tried to push off the bedcovers. It wasn't often there was a heatwave in Brighton, but there must be one now, because she was stifling under the tarpaulin cover of a sailing dinghy she had just sold to a short, fat man and she couldn't get out. She heard him talking to someone else.

'How long has she been like this?' the fat man asked.

'I felt sure she would be all right after resting in bed all day. I hope you made her stay in bed—I gave Benita strict instructions.'

'Benita vanished before I came home, and Minella is not a young lady who'll be ordered about. She got up for dinner.'

'Tch, tch, tch! No wonder she has a fever! She should have been kept as quiet as possible and only given light food. I suppose you gave her steak!'

'Pork and sausage, actually, but she didn't eat much.'

The fat man threw up his hands in horror. 'No, no, no, that is terrible!'

'I'm sorry, Henrique. Vasco Hernandez came up

here, which didn't help matters. You know how I feel about him.'

'I suppose you shouted and frightened her. Is that what happened?'

'No, a little thing like that wouldn't frighten Minella,' said Sam. 'She was all right until I had to tell her about the yacht breaking up. Her brother was on it, and I think they must have been very close. She keeps calling for him.'

'Yes,' agreed Dr Porva, 'it is very sad. Very sad. Now, I will give her something to bring down the fever and make her sleep naturally, and I insist she must not be disturbed. You are bad for a young, innocent girl, *o men amigo.*'

When Minella woke up the room was cool. The curtains were pulled across the window to keep out the sun and her skin felt dry again, no longer bathed in perspiration. She lifted her arms above the sheets and found she was once more wearing the voluminous nightgown, and she wondered how it had been put on without her knowing.

Seeing a movement in the bed, a plump, dark woman who had been knitting in the corner came over and looked at her, and when she saw Minella was awake her face lit up.

'Ah, you are better! The fever, he has gone.'

Minella frowned, not recognising her immediately. What was a foreign woman doing in her bedroom? And then she remembered.

'Benita, why did you put your nightdress back on me? It's much too big.'

Benita finished the row of knitting and prodded both needles through a large ball of wool.

'I did not do it. Sam, he put it on. It is my best one.'

Minella glanced round the room and saw the jeans and shirt she had been wearing neatly folded and hanging on the back of a chair. He must have taken those off her first. Her face coloured and Benita quickly put a hand to her forehead to test for a temperature.

'You weren't here last night,' Minella said to her. 'Did you come over this morning?'

'I came yesterday. All day I looked after you.'

'Yesterday? How long have I been here?'

'Two days,' said Benita.

Minella closed her eyes and turned her head away. All at once she remembered what Sam had told her just before she collapsed, and an ache spread right through her body, worse than anything she had ever known. In front of her stretched a vast emptiness and she wished she could sleep on and on and know nothing more about it. Both Greg and Annette were dead and there was no one else in her life who mattered.

She didn't want to talk, and when Benita chattered in her broken English she pretended not to hear. The present was so painful she couldn't cope with it yet, and all she could do was let her mind wander through the past where there had been happiness.

It was Greg who taught her to sail. Living by the sea and with all the facilities within easy reach, he spent most of his spare time with boats, and because Minella was often with him he took pride in coaching her so that she was able to take part in dinghy racing at a very early age. Her mother was delighted, not by her daughter's achievement, but because she became so absorbed in sailing she was hardly ever at home. As soon as school was out she was down at the harbour, and at weekends she was too occupied with boats to bother about doing homework, until her teachers complained and Greg scolded her. Her mother didn't even bother to look at her report.

Without Greg her childhood might not have been so happy. Patricia Farmer was not the maternal type and Minella had been a mistake, but with her husband's help it might have been fun bringing up a daughter. When he died soon after the baby's birth she was heartbroken, and acted as if Minella was to blame. Patricia rejected her. And Greg, who was then ten years old, found himself having to stay in and look after his tiny sister more and more often. He accepted the situation stoically. Aware that his mother was making new friends and didn't want to be bothered with the baby, he took responsibility for Minella, and it was to him she turned for much of her love and affection.

Patricia Farmer was a frivolous woman in many ways, but she had a good head for business, and with the help of one of her new friends she opened an antique shop. She dressed impeccably, and as Minella grew older and showed signs of becoming a very attractive girl, she enjoyed buying her expensive clothes. It was as if she was dressing a doll. What she couldn't give her in the way of love she tried to make up for with money, but Minella never had any illusions. She was a nuisance to her mother. Greg was nearly old enough to be off her hands, but she was saddled with Minella for many years yet.

But though Patricia had little time for her daughter, the ties with her son grew stronger, and soon after leaving college she had drawn him into the antiques business. She resented it when he was at the sailing club, and involved him in discussions about hallmarks and glazing until he was as enthusiastic about antiques as she had intended him to be. Minella watched him growing stuffier and less fun to be with, too much in his mother's company, and she worried about him. Some instinct beyond her years warned her that her mother was using him to compensate for her own loneliness, yet she refused to turn to Minella who needed her love so badly.

She was fifteen when she met Annette Moran. Annette joined the staff of Minella's school when she was in the fourth year, and they were drawn together by recognition of a loneliness each thought was well hidden. Minella was happy at school, but she had never encouraged close friendships, as the older girl discovered when both sought the same retreat on several consecutive dinner hours. They began to talk and found they shared mutual interests, sailing among them, and it was not long before Minella invited her to the sailing club. Friendship grew between them in spite of the difference in their ages, and she liked Annette more than any girl she had ever met. More than anything she wanted her to meet her brother.

'You'll like Greg,' she had said. 'He's the most wonderful brother in all the world.'

'I'm sure he is,' said Annette.

But she was in no hurry to meet him, and it was soon obvious she was putting forward every excuse to avoid it. Minella was hurt, but on one rare occasion when they were talking of personal things Annette spoke of her past.

'I don't trust men any more. The one I was going to marry ran out on me, and I'd loved him more than anyone on earth. We'd made such marvellous plans for the future, but everything changed when he was injured and lost his job. It made no difference to the way I felt, but he was very bitter and he didn't want me any more. I was ready to give up everything for him, but he went off without a word and I've never heard from him again. It was *so* cruel.'

Minella's young, romantic heart ached for her. How could anyone walk out on a girl as beautiful as Annette, so poised and tall and blonde? With youthful fervour she declared that if ever she came across the man she would tell him exactly what she thought of such despicable behaviour. How Annette had laughed!

'Well, Greg would never do an awful thing like that,' Minella had declared. 'When you meet him you'll know all men are not worthless. You'll love him, just like I do.'

And that was how it was, except that Annette loved him enough to say she would marry him. It had brought Minella a little closer to her mother, who had resented the marriage bitterly at first, but there was no one as dear to her as her brother and his wife.

Now she would never see either of them again, and her grief was too deep for tears. She felt completely empty, devoid of all emotion, and all she could do was stare at the blank wall until sleep mercifully claimed her once more.

The next day she was stronger. In the night she had woken up to hear rain beating on the window, and the sound of it had unleashed a flood of tears which she had shed almost silently until all her crying was done. She was alone now and in a foreign land where no one would want to be burdened with her sorrow, so the sooner she picked up the pieces and faced her situation the easier it would be. There was no one to fight her battles, no one to give her advice, and she was answerable to no one but herself. For a moment the outlook was too bleak to contemplate, but Minella alway faced life bravely, and the practice she had had stood her in good stead.

As soon as it was light she got up and dressed in the sweat-shirt and jeans she had been wearing when she was rescued. Benita had washed them for her. Then she walked out into the garden on shaky legs which didn't seem to belong to her.

The air was beautiful and the smell of the earth after rain reminded her of the park in Brighton. But nothing was less like Brighton than the breathtaking view of the lake, like a jewel amidst the lush green vegetation and scintillating as a diamond in the early morning sun.

At the edge of the garden was a fence where bougainvillaea splashed red and purple disguise over the old wooden panels, and as she walked beside it she came unexpectedly upon a path that dropped steeply away from the cultivated spread of lawn and flowers. She stood at the narrow opening, so well hidden that only close inspection revealed it was there, and was lured by the pull of secrecy it suggested. The path itself

was not overgrown. Once past the concealed divide it
widened out and steps had been cut at intervals to make
the going easier. Minella took it slowly, wishing she had
her normal bouncing energy, for she would have loved
to take the steep descent at a run, but by the time she
reached the bottom she was so tired she wondered how
she would find the strength for the climb back. She
must have been out of her mind to attempt it, but she
had never been able to resist exploring interesting
places. This time it hardly seemed worth the effort.
There was only the lake and a grove of trees that looked
like beech, the leaves still catching the pink tints of an
Azorean dawn.

Then she saw the little stone building beyond the
trees, and straight away curiosity conquered all physical
weakness. The path now led down below the tree line
and she followed it until she was almost at the water's
edge and was walking over a greyish-black sand. The
hut was to the right and she came to it just as the sun
rose high enough to shine on creeper-covered walls
where the flowers were as big as trumpets, and would
go on bathing it in light until it was well past its zenith.

It was very warm already, and she hadn't realised
how exhausted she was, but having reached her goal she
would not be beaten until she had seen what was inside
the hut. It was a squat, square building with just one
room, and the wooden door was locked. The single
window was fairly high, but by standing on tiptoe she
could just glimpse the interior where the sun shone like
a spotlight into one corner. Then she sank back on her
heels and gradually down to the ground until she was
leaning against the wall, and she was very puzzled by
what she had seen.

Canvases. Yes, that was what they were. Large
paintings, some of them in frames, were stored here,
packed together and stacked in the corner in all
innocence, because no one would be suspicious of a
picturesque hut by the lakeside even if they knew of its

existence. Minella was suddenly so hot she had to move into the shade. She had stumbled upon a mystery, she was convinced of it, and she was not sure whether she wanted to investigate any further.

Her head was spinning and she pressed her fingers to her temples, trying to recall fragments of conversation, but time plays strange tricks and she was separated from those memories by shock and fever which made it difficult to know how long ago it was she had spoken to Vasco. If only her mind was clearer! Perhaps she was imagining things. Vasco had said that Sam didn't like being asked questions, hinting that there were things in his past he didn't want known. Surely she hadn't dreamed it.

She closed her eyes and remembered how Sam had shouted when he found Benita had brought her to the house. He definitely hadn't wanted her there, and he hadn't wanted Vasco either. In fact he didn't want anyone trespassing on his solitude, with the exception of Benita herself whom he needed to cook for him and keep his house in order, and who was probably too trusting to have any doubts about him anyway.

Sam Stafford was a very mysterious man, and the more Minella thought about it the more convinced she became he had a lot to hide. It wasn't natural to guard his privacy the way he did, objecting to visitors and cutting himself off from the world. He didn't seem to have an occupation, so what did he live on? The house was not luxurious, but he had everything he wanted and some of the ornaments around looked costly as far as Minella could tell with her limited knowledge of values. And he had to pay Benita a wage. He was cultured, too. His voice was low and attractive, the accent pure, and just hearing it in her mind made her pause and wonder if she should reconsider her suspicions. But criminals could be very gullible, and on the level she was beginning to class him it was likely he came from an intellectual background. She had read about art thefts.

No amateur would get away with the type of crime she saw emerging. Sam Stafford could be involved in thefts worth millions of pounds if those canvases were works of art. How clever of him to have gone to ground in such an idyllic spot!

Perhaps it would have been better if she hadn't followed the path down to the lake. If this really was a hiding place for stolen treasure it must never be known that she had discovered it. Her life might even be in danger. She leaned her head back against the stonework and closed her eyes, a peculiar fluttering sensation upsetting her stomach.

She didn't want Sam to be a man in exile, unable to return to his own country for fear of detection. He affected her strangely, excited her, yet made her angry with his arrogant manner, and she knew she must get away from him as soon as possible, though where she would go she had no idea. Anywhere would be better than staying in his house now that she was beset by such terrible doubts.

She must get back to the garden before anyone missed her. It would never do for Benita to raise an alarm when she came in with breakfast and found the bedroom empty. She got to her feet and felt dizzy, but after a moment it passed and she took a few uncertain steps. Then an overwhelming itch to take one more peep inside the hut made her turn and stand again on tiptoe at the window.

Her nose was still pressed to the window when Sam's angry voice made her stiffen with fright.

'What the hell are you doing down here? Get down from there this minute!'

His feet hadn't made a sound on the soft black sand and he was behind her before she had a chance to escape.

'I couldn't stay in bed any longer,' she said, sliding round to face him, and she clasped her hands in front of her like a schoolgirl caught misbehaving. She looked very small and young, her brown hair falling across her forehead in a fringe which almost obscured her vision, and she licked her top lip nervously.

'You must be mad, girl! Getting up from a sickbed and coming this far! I knew I couldn't trust you.'

'Oh, but you can,' she interrupted swiftly. 'The view was so beautiful I just had to come down to the lake, and then I wondered if anyone lived in the hut.'

'You're an interfering brat, too nosey for your own good,' he stormed. 'And you deserve to be ill again. When I went in the bedroom and found you weren't there I couldn't believe it!'

Her eyes flashed. 'You shouldn't have come into my bedroom.' She didn't know how appealing she looked with her pale cheeks and wide, innocent eyes.

'The room is mine,' he reminded her. 'And as I've helped nurse you through a fever and sat with you while you were delirious you could say I'm getting used to seeing you in bed, so there's no need for you to object. You've no sense at all.' He towered over her and she wanted to get away, but the wall was behind her. 'Now I'll carry you back.'

'You'll do no such thing!' Minella shouted. 'I walked down here, and I'll walk back, thank you very much!'

The sun was in her eyes and she squinted at him, swaying a little. He reached out to steady her, but she darted away, terrified he might touch her. Summoning all her strength, she made for the path and concentrated on each step, knowing that he would follow her. The climb was as daunting as Everest, but she wouldn't give in. Sam was close on her heels and it was a cat-and-mouse game as she scrambled up the path, afraid he would catch her if she hesitated.

She tripped just before she reached the entrance to the garden at the top, and Sam took hold of her. He drew her back against him like a child who had run away, and she kicked and struggled, and bit the arm that pinioned her to him.

'Let me go!' she screamed. 'I hate you! Let me go!'

He didn't move, resisting her attack with rock-like firmness, but she felt him take a deep, angry breath. 'You're going to need my help, Minella, in a day or two when you're strong enough to face the future. Don't reject me out of hand or you might regret it.'

When he let her go she fled into the garden, across the lawn and into the house, which was still as peaceful as when she left it. Her heart was thudding painfully and she gasped for breath as she clung to the doorpost. She could see the bedroom across the way and her body ached with the need to lie down, but the bed was Sam's and she couldn't use it any more. After a minute she had recovered enough to go through to the patio, intending to rest on the sun-bed, but his clothes were there and the blanket he had been using. She felt trapped. Wherever she turned there was Sam Stafford, and she wanted to get away from him. Perspiration gathered under the fringe on her forehead, and yet she felt cold. The bedroom beckoned like a sanctuary and she returned to it reluctantly, going inside and shutting the door.

Sam knocked before he came in, and by then the sun was high.

'I've brought you a belated breakfast,' he said, setting down a tray of food. 'Benita was late arriving. Her father's needs were greater than yours this morning.'

He didn't wait for an answer but went out again before she could even thank him. His abruptness made her stubborn and she contemplated pushing the tray away and not eating anything, but she was hungry and Benita had made it look tempting.

When Sam returned she was standing by the window, not daring to look at him. He filled her with such complex emotions she couldn't begin to sort them out, and she was so tense there was cramp in her shoulders. He shut the door and came and stood beside her.

'So you think the lake is beautiful,' he said.

She relaxed a little. She could handle things on an

ordinary conversational level, and it sounded as if he had calmed down.

'Yes, I do,' she agreed. 'It's so peaceful it looks like a picture on a calendar. You're very lucky to live in a place like this.'

He glanced at her, then away again. 'Appearances can be deceptive. That tranquil beauty is only on the surface. What lies underneath is literally fire and brimstone, and there's no knowing when it might show its temper.'

'I don't understand,' she said.

'The Azores are volcanic islands,' he explained. 'That lake is the crater of a volcano and the black sand you were walking on is lava that it once threw up. Sometimes it grumbles. I hope it never erupts again.'

She was fascinated and turned to him eagerly. 'You think it might?'

'It's not impossible. This island is famous for its eruptions. In 1957 there was such a terrible one a whole new island burst up out of the sea like a furnace and disappeared again two weeks later. Most people were evacuated, but those that stayed on slept out in the open because villages were destroyed by the violent tremors. Nearly a year they lasted. I wish I'd been here then.'

She took a fresh look at the lake surrounded by verdant green hillside and was amazed, especially when he told her even the cattle had been transported to Portugal because there was not enough grass left to feed them.

'I can't believe it,' she murmured. Yet hadn't she felt disturbance the other night in the garden even though there was none? 'It looks as if nothing has changed for centuries. How could anything so beautiful be so cruel?'

'You tell me,' said Sam.

He let the words linger between them, full of hidden meaning which eluded her initially. When his eyes met hers they were questioning, glinting with a cynical humour that challenged her to find an answer.

'I take it you're trying to make some clever comparison,' she said coldly, determined not to flinch from that shrewd gaze.

'You and the lake have certain things in common. You're a lovely girl and you look serene when you're asleep. But I've glimpsed the fire underneath, and it intrigues me.'

Her head began to reel as she sensed approaching involvement with this man which had to be prevented at all costs. The sparks he saw were of his own creating, for she had never been so physically aware of another person in her life, and a flame had been ignited from the very beginning, but if he was hoping to evoke some kind of passionate response he was in for a disappointment.

'If you're hoping I'll be a push-over, Mr Stafford, you're very much mistaken. I may be out in the wilds, but I've got very high principles and I'll stick to them!'

His lips twitched, and then to her dismay he threw back his head and laughed.

'My, but you flatter yourself, little one,' he said, catching hold of her hands. 'I was referring to the display of temper I was treated to earlier this morning. My shins are still suffering!'

Colour crept into her cheeks. 'I'm sorry. I'm afraid I've had to be independent all my life.'

The amusement faded from his eyes, replaced by compassion as he saw pain gathering at the memory.

'Minella, I've got to ask you some questions,' he said. 'You haven't been fit until now and I don't know anything about you except your name and the yacht you were on. You've no papers ... nothing, so I haven't been able to contact your family. We must let your mother know you're safe.'

She lifted her chin and was even more on the defensive. 'My mother wouldn't be interested.'

'What a dreadful thing to say!'

'But it's true. She married again three years ago and

went to live in New Zealand. I only hear from her at Christmas.' She extricated her hands and turned away so that he couldn't witness the misery she felt at telling him. 'She'll be heartbroken about Greg, though. He was the one she cared about.' She paused again, then faced him anxiously. 'Please, have they ... have they found him yet? Shall I have to go and identify him? Oh, I don't think I could bear it!'

'Only two bodies have been washed up so far,' he told her, his tone deliberately impersonal. 'Both have been identified and have no connection with you. The strange thing is the authorities can't even find your name among any of the crew lists.'

'I don't suppose they can,' she said. 'I replaced someone who dropped out at the last minute. But let me assure you I'm not a spy.'

Now why on earth had she said that? Those silly suspicions she'd had down by the hut were surely just a product of the delirium she'd been suffering from, and he'd only laugh again if he knew. She was tired and unhappy, and she wished he would go away.

'Why do you hate me, Sparrow?' he asked. 'What have I done to deserve it?'

The question was unexpected and she was caught off guard. 'Did I say that?'

'You did.'

He looked quite upset about it, though she knew it was only play-acting and it brought a smile. But he had a right to ask, because he'd given her food and shelter yet she'd shown no gratitude. Greg would have been ashamed of her. It was midday and very hot, and she felt a desperate need for air. She reached up to release the catch on the window and pushed it open, but Sam leaned over her and closed it again before the slightest breeze could stir the curtains.

'You'll let the heat in if you do that. Better to close the shutters if you want it cool.'

She hadn't noticed the slatted shutters behind the

curtains until he folded them slowly into place and the room was dimmed. He had slipped an arm casually round her shoulder and waves of heat which had nothing to do with the temperature outside radiated through her. In the half-light his profile was silhouetted, emphasising the aristocratic set of his head, and a choking feeling caught at her throat. It was bad enough being near him in daylight, but the intimacy evoked by the closed shutters was too much for her and she gave a startled cry. Sam looked at her, smiling at her timidity, and before she could avoid it his mouth came down gently on hers. The kiss was feather-soft on her lips and set them quivering, and it awakened sensations of such extraordinary sweetness she closed her eyes and was tempted to press herself against him for the comfort she needed. But his grip on her tightened as he became aware of her response, and she took fright. With a gasp, she twisted her head away.

'Oh, no, you don't!' she cried. 'I don't know who or what you are, and I don't want to find out. You've been alone too long, but you won't take advantage of *me*. Your friends weren't doing you a service when they dropped me in your bed, because I'll never give in to you. You're a lecherous devil, that's why I hate you. Oh, how I wish my brother was here instead of you!'

She pounded his chest with her fists so hard his shoulders rounded to ward off the attack, but he kept hold of her and a look of disbelief changed rapidly to anger. Powerful arms crushed her against him until there was no room left to fight, and then he kissed her again, brutally. He forced open her lips and bruised them, and this time she felt nothing but revulsion, her body becoming rigid with fear. There was no escape from the cruel, damaging pressure of that kiss until her fingers came in contact with his beard, and she pulled it with all the strength she had left. He let her go so abruptly she fell sideways on the bed.

'I'm *not* your brother, Minella, so don't expect me to

treat you the way *he* did,' he grated, fury giving weight to each word. 'Remember that!'

He left her there without another glance and strode out of the room. A few minutes later she heard his car start up and rattle over the rough driveway down to the road.

CHAPTER FOUR

'BENITA! Benita!'

Minella called through the house, but no one answered and she began to think she must be alone. She didn't know how far it was to the nearest town and had no recollection of how far she had come from the village where she had been picked up, but she had to get away from Sam's place. Without any money she didn't know what she was going to do, or where she could go. Her legs hardly felt like carrying her any great distance.

She called Benita again, and heard a clatter from the kitchen. Of course, it was separated from the rest of the house by that funny passage. Minella hurried along it and found Benita making bread.

'Benita, please can you find Vasco for me?' she said. I must see him straight away.'

The Azorean woman slapped dough on to a floured board and pounded it with such force it looked as if she, too, had had a bad morning and was finding an outlet in vigorous kneading.

'What for you want my nephew? He is not allowed here.'

'I know, but I've got to get away, and he's the only one who'll help me.'

Benita snorted. 'Hmm! He only help himself, that one.' She looked at Minella curiously, pushing her sleeves further up her floury arms. 'Why for you want to run away?'

The oven made it very hot in the kitchen and perspiration trickled down Minella's back, soaking her shirt. She didn't know how anyone could work in such heat.

'I've *got* to leave before Sam gets back, and I don't know where to go,' she explained.

There was a long-handled implement by the wall which Benita picked up and used like a shovel to deposit rounded lumps of dough into the dark recess of the oven. Then she turned again to Minella.

'Why? Did he make love to you?'

'No, he did not!' Minella cried indignantly. It was a terrible thing to suggest and she had sounded quite casual, as if talking about the weather. What made it worse was the knowledge it could so easily have happened if she hadn't fought against him, and she had an awful suspicion that Benita might have known what was going on. It was humiliating.

'Then what is the trouble?' Benita asked, in all innocence. 'Sam is a very nice man. Maybe you are cross because he *not* make love to you.'

'Oh!' Minella gasped, bereft of words. The woman was prejudiced. It didn't matter that Sam Stafford treated her nephew badly and had a boorish lack of manners. He was her employer and she was definitely on his side. Or was she more than that to him? Perhaps she was jealous. 'You can stop making silly remarks, Benita. I hardly know the man, and he doesn't want me here any more than I want to stay. And anyway, I must go into town and find out a lot of things ... like how am I going to get to England without any means of paying the fare.'

'Sam, he will lend you money.'

'I couldn't possibly ask him.'

He hadn't offered any financial help and Minella had been too embarrassed to speak of it. The cost of an airline ticket would be quite considerable and she couldn't expect him to fork out for one without any guarantee that he would get his money back. No, the place to go was the British Embassy, supposing there was one on this island. Come to that, there might not even be an airport. She knew very little about the

Azores. All at once she felt very lonely and lost, stranded on a tiny strip of land in the middle of the Atlantic with nothing of her own except the pair of jeans and shirt she stood up in.

Benita wiped the flour off her hands with her apron, then took off the apron, rolled it up and threw it on to the table. There was concern in her dark eyes and she wagged a finger at the young girl who had blown into her life like a piece of thistledown.

'I think you are afraid of Sam,' she said.

'Yes,' Minella admitted, 'I think I am.'

It was true. Sam's personality was too powerful. She had never met anyone like him before, and nervousness made her say and do impulsive things that wouldn't cross her mind any other time.

Suddenly Benita was overcome with Latin emotion and tears collected in her eyes. 'It is sad. Once he was going to marry, but the lady, she left him. He never forget her, but maybe he could if someone else came to love him.'

'Well, don't go expecting it to be me!' Minella was alarmed. 'I don't want any more to do with him.'

'Poof!' scoffed Benita, flouncing back to the oven. 'You are too young anyway.'

'And *he* wouldn't look so old without that beard,' Minella retorted. 'Now I'm going.'

She retraced her steps through the passage and went to the bedroom again, though she didn't know why. There was nothing for her to pack. She stared at the windows with the closed shutters, took a gulping breath, then pushed them aside with determination so that sunlight flooded in and washed away the memory of what had taken place there, for the moment at least.

Benita had followed her.

'He will not forgive me if I let you go. You have been ill.' Her voice was contrite, and when Minella looked round she held out motherly arms in a beseeching gesture that was hard to resist.

'But I'm better now. You can say you didn't know I'd gone.'

'Where you go?'

'I told you, Vasco will help me,' Minella said.

She wished she had something to carry. The very fact that she had nothing seemed to emphasise her dependence on other people, and though she wasn't aware of it there was a hint of panic in her voice.

'I no understand the English,' said Benita, with a shake of her head. 'You are so cold. And you always hurry. Why you not sit here and wait?'

'What would I wait for?'

The older woman lifted her shoulders and spread her fingers. 'I no know. Maybe your brother will come back.'

The irony of it almost made Minella weep and she couldn't understand the logic of such a remark. She was sure Benita wouldn't be deliberately cruel. Her eyes were still soulful.

'My brother is dead,' she explained softly.

'How you know?' Benita demanded. '*You* were saved from the sea. Why not him also?'

For a moment Minella couldn't speak. Her hand went to her throat and a fluttering of hope, too fragile to grasp, made her swallow hard. 'Oh, Benita,' she whispered, 'do you really think it might be possible?'

The expressive shoulders lifted again. 'I no know. Maybe.' Then she held out her arms once more and this time Minella ran to her, welcoming the feel of that wonderful, motherly embrace with eagerness, having never known much maternal affection. 'There, there, my child,' Benita crooned, 'it will be all right.'

It *was* only a remote chance, and perhaps it was unwise to even consider it when her hopes could be finally dashed at any hour, but she had always been an optimist and while there was no definite news she could still believe in miracles.

Nothing was real. She didn't know exactly how long

she'd been here, for at least two days were lost in the mists of fever, but during that time Greg had seemed very close. She hadn't fully accepted that she would never see him again. Perhaps the shock was too recent for her to absorb it, because even the tears she had shed through the night had been partly to assuage the hopelessness of her own plight. She had no thought beyond the present, and realised she didn't know what day of the week it was. What harm could there be in clinging to a dream for a little while longer?

A dusting of flour coated Benita's warm brown skin, but the comforting smell of baking was almost lost beneath the heavy perfume she applied liberally and allowed to remain indefinitely. Minella extricated herself from the embrace and it was obvious she was not going to be content to sit and wait for anything. Benita's attempt at delaying her had had just the opposite effect. Her determination to leave was stronger than ever.

'Oh, Benita, now I've *got* to find my way to town,' she explained. 'Don't you see, I've got to make different enquiries from the ones Sam made. I must see the right people. Greg might be on one of the other islands. Perhaps he's alive and feeling as desolate as I am because they've told him *I* was drowned.' She gave her an impetuous hug. 'Oh, it's even more important I get away from here now.'

Benita sighed. 'All right, all right. But I am not happy.' She swung round as if she washed her hands of the whole affair, but plumped herself in the doorway, successfully hindering an immediate escape. 'First you rest. It is siesta . . . much too hot for you to walk even a little way. Later I will bring you milk and some food, then I tell how you get to my house.'

Two hours later Minella felt like Dick Whittington setting off on his travels with all his possessions tied in a scarf, except that the scarf Benita had given her was tied round her head to keep off the sun, and the food in the bundle was for Vasco and his grandfather. Benita had come with her as far as the end of the driveway and pointed out a white house in the distance which she assured her was nearer than it looked. She also had strict instructions to tell Vasco to bring her back by nightfall, but though she hadn't argued she had no intention of returning to Sam's house. He'd been kind, but only because he had no alternative, and she would write and thank him when she finally reached home.

The road was narrow and lined with bushes, most of them the ubiquitous blue hydrangeas which coloured the landscape like patches of material left over from the spread of clear blue sky. To her left there was an orange grove with high stone walls to protect the crop from Atlantic gales, and there was shade until the walls gave way to open meadow. Five minutes' more walking and she guessed she would reach the Hernandez house, but already she felt as exhausted as if she had spent hours struggling across a desert and was parched with the heat. Before attempting to cross the meadow she sank down in the shade and gazed at the view.

Benita had told her the name of the island was Fayal, and that from her father's house you could see another island called Pico. She had been walking downhill, and now she was clear of the orange grove she saw a narrow channel of water separating the two islands, and on the far side was a mountain which dominated everything. It looked like a volcano, but it's beauty shimmered in the heat haze with dreamlike tranquillity which made it appear incapable of anger, as did the sea when it widened out into a vast expanse of ocean. The colour of sea and sky was indivisible, the horizon no more than a smudge, and as Minella stared at the water for the first time since the night of the storm she could hardly believe how terrifying it had been. And now that she was alone her brave hopes for Greg faded. The odds against survival after the yacht broke up were stacked high, and any good news would surely have filtered through to Sam.

Her eyelids were heavy and drowsiness made her too limp to move, but she had to reach the house across the meadow. She looked up as a flock of small birds flew over and settled in a nearby tree. To her amazement she saw they were green canaries, and the birdsong that filled the air was so sweet it seemed meant to lift her spirits. She got to her feet with renewed determination not to let anything beat her.

The single-storeyed house where Benita's family lived was much the same size as Sam's, similarly whitewashed and roofed with terracotta-coloured tiles. A gate stood open and a deeply rutted track made by ox-carts led up to an open-fronted barn where maize was drying. There was no one around. The side wall of the house was completely covered with vines and it seemed as if crops grew right to the door, freshly turned ground showing that every square inch was precious. Minella wandered round to the other side where two pigs were penned and chickens squawked at the sight of a stranger, but still no one came and she wondered if only the old man with the trouble-some heart was at home, until a young man appeared who looked very much like Vasco.

'Hello,' said Minella. 'I'm trying to find Vasco. Is he here? Benita sent me.'

He opened his mouth in surprise, then spoke in rapid Portuguese. She laughed and shook her head to show she didn't understand, and when she held out the bundle of food he didn't know whether to take it until he recognised the wrapping.

'Vasco,' Minella repeated, seeing it was useless to say anything else.

'Ah si,' said the young man, and went off indoors.

She was left standing in the sun, not knowing whether to follow him, and there was a nervous ache in her legs. After his reception at Sam's the other night perhaps Vasco had changed his mind about wanting to see her. She couldn't blame him if he had, but who else was there? She couldn't go any further without transport, that was certain.

Waves of desolation threatened to break over her as she stood there, but were averted when Vasco appeared from quite a different quarter. He had been in the barn, and on seeing her he gave a yell of delight. He sprang over a low fence and placed himself in front of her, hands on hips, triumph lighting him with exhilaration.

'You have come!'

He was poised like a dancer, a beaming smile of welcome aimed at her with dynamic effect. She was dazzled.

'Y-es,' she said hesitantly. It wasn't often she was lost for words, but while he looked at her with such flattering fascination she was speechless.

'I have won a bet,' he said. 'Benita told me I behaved so badly you would never want to see me again, but here you are. I have won!'

He struck his chest with his fist victoriously, and Minella felt instantly deflated. Her coming had done wonders for his ego, which was more important than being pleased to see her for her own sake.

'You're quite incorrigible,' she said, with English primness that baffled him. The word was new, but the meaning clear. She hadn't come because she found him irresistible, so there must be some other reason. He tried to look suitably chastised, but the light of excitement continued to burn.

'I am sorry. Let me get you a drink and we will sit in the shade and talk.'

'I'd like a glass of water, please,' said Minella.

'Water? Pah, what is that? I will bring you something much better.'

He took her to the barn where it was cooler, and the smell of drying maize was so agreeable she gave a sniff of pleasure, but she was wary of the enclosed space.

'Vasco, please will you take me to Horta. I'm so

muddled I don't know where to start sorting things out, but Benita says that's the best place.'

'For you, my beautiful one, I will do anything,' he said. 'First a drink, and then I will get my motorbike.'

'Oh, no! I've never been on a motorbike.'

'And I have no car, so it is the only way I can take you to Horta. Why did you not ask Sam?'

That was something Minella preferred not to talk about, so she hurriedly agreed to risk riding pillion as long as he promised not to go too fast.

'I will drive ver-y slowly,' he said. 'That way we will be very close for a long time.'

He gave an audacious smile that spoke volumes and slipped away before she could say any more. Whatever was the matter with the men here? She was beginning to think there was nothing to choose between Sam and Vasco, but on consideration she decided Vasco's open flirting was preferable to Sam's insidious attempts at seduction, and she was lucky she had come out of the final humiliation easily. Ever since it happened she had been trying not to think about the force he had used when he kissed her. If he'd been intent on raping her there wouldn't have been much she could do to stop him. That strength could have overpowered her in seconds. She shuddered. There was no question of why she was leaving. It most certainly wouldn't have been safe to stay.

Vasco returned with a jug of wine and two thick tumblers, one of which he filled and handed to her.

'This will revive you,' he said. 'It is good. I am told the Tsar of Russia once used to drink our wine.'

She sipped it, and found he wasn't exaggerating. It was the best wine she had ever tasted. 'It's lovely,' she said. 'Where do you get it?'

'See, the vines.' He gave an expansive wave to indicate the wall where vines grew thickly, almost covering the window. 'We make it.'

She drank a little more and it was so refreshing she quickly emptied the tumbler. There couldn't be much harm in home-brewed wine. For the first time since leaving Sam's she began to relax and a warm feeling of complacency stole over her. All she'd needed to put things right was to get away from his environment.

'My name's Minella,' she told Vasco. 'I don't think anyone told you.'

'Minella.' He tested the name thoughtfully, then smiled. 'Yes, I like it.'

'Now can we go to Horta? There's such a lot I've got to do.'

Vasco leaned back on one elbow and surveyed her with obvious appreciation. He wore a dark blue shirt with the collar turned up to keep the sun off his neck and it was opened nearly to the waist. His smooth brown chest glistened. With confidence inspired by the wine Minella found herself returning his look of appraisal, but realised the danger as soon as he moved a fraction closer. Friendship was quite definitely all she required of him, and she sat up very straight with her back to the drying maize, making it clear she didn't fancy him the way he hoped.

'Why are you in such a hurry?' he asked. 'Always the English are in a hurry.'

She laughed. 'That's what Benita said. You just copied from her.' She paused, letting him catch the rebuke, but a flicker of the eyes warned her he wouldn't take kindly to teasing, and as she was dependent on him for the moment she had to make amends. 'Who taught you to speak such good English?'

Mollified, he said: 'Sam. He taught me.'

His answer surprised her, because she had expected him to say Benita. In order to learn so well he would have had to spend a lot of time in Sam's company.

'But I thought you and Sam didn't like each other,' she said.

'Not now. There was ... how you say ... a misunderstand.' He stood up and brushed dried maize husks from his jeans.

Minella was intrigued. Everything about Sam was secretive, and even though she hoped not to see him again her curiosity hadn't abated.

'Tell me about it,' she urged.

'It would take too long,' said Vasco, 'and you are in a hurry.' He gave a smug grin and picked up the two tumblers. 'Come, my motorbike is at the front.'

She followed him round the side of the house, as annoyed as he had been at the hint of teasing and frustrated at still not being able to find out anything about Sam. It was not that she was interested in the man, but it was like reading a mystery novel with the last pages missing.

At the front of the house the young man Minella had seen first was working in a vegetable patch as beautiful as a flower garden. Vasco called him and they shouted across in Portuguese to each other.

'That is my brother Enrico. He works here with our grandfather.'

'And do you do farming too?' she asked.

'No. I go out with the whaleboats,' he said. 'Now, I get something from the house and then we will go to Horta.'

It was a journey Minella would never forget. As instructed she clasped her arms round Vasco's waist and clung on fearfully as he sped along the narrow roads. Bracken and hortensia hedge brushed against her legs, and a skirmish with an ox-cart brought down a shower of barley in her hair. And the noise of the ancient machine, of which Vasco was so proud, actually drowned the screech of the ox-cart axles. Women in a field stopped tying sacks of grain and shaded their eyes to see if the noise came from the sky or the road, and an old man brandished a pitchfork when Vasco swerved out to avoid him.

'I must stop at Santa Silva,' he called over his shoulder, and dropped his speed to drive down through a village which Minella guessed was the one where she had been brought ashore. The cottages seemed one on top of the other, white walls dazzling in the sunlight, but hardly anyone was around. At the bottom of the hill Vasco stopped, called out a greeting to a woman in black who carried a basket on her head, and jumped off the bike so quickly Minella overbalanced. He laughed and steadied her.

'I have to go round the bay to see whether the boat will go out tonight. You can walk down to the sea, or visit Dr Porva if he is there. I shall not be long.'

The sun was getting low, but it was still very hot and she was shattered by the ride. It felt as if every bone in her body had been tossed in a bag and banged against a wall. And she had no idea how much further it was to Horta. She was beginning to think they would arrive there too late to do anything, added to which was the worry of where she was going to spend the night. In the rush to get away from Sam she had made no plans other than to try and reach an Embassy. If there wasn't one perhaps the police could help her. Or Dr Porva.

'I think I'll visit the doctor,' she said. 'Which is his house?'

Vasco put out his hand and touched the stonework beside them. 'This one. I will come back for you here.'

When he had gone she was too nervous to knock on the door. Twice the doctor had cared for her, yet she had forgotten what he looked like. All she could remember was his voice and the way he had panted for breath coming up the cliff from the beach, and from these she had formed the picture of a round, genial Dickensian character which was probably nothing like reality. Perhaps he wouldn't want to see her after she'd been such a nuisance, but at least she could thank him.

Two children were staring at her. Strangers were rare in Santa Silva and when she spoke to them in English they laughed and ran away, kicking a ball as they went. Wishing she was as carefree as they were, Minella plucked up courage and tapped the door, but no one came. The doctor was out.

Vasco had disappeared down a road at the side of the

house and with nothing else to do she turned the same corner, finding herself on a shingle path that led down to the shore. She could see the sea some distance away, gentle breakers curling on to black sand in a horseshoe-shaped bay, and she knew this was the hill up which Sam had carried her, though she hadn't imagined it looking like this. There was a peculiar tightness in her chest at the thought of him bearing her to safety like Perseus rescuing Andromeda from the sea monster. If it hadn't been such a perilous situation, the way he took charge would have had quite a romantic touch. Pity he hadn't followed through.

She walked a little way further, drawn towards the shore by morbid fascination. It was a fishing village and boats were drawn up high as though they were expecting more bad weather, but the sky was clear and not even a breeze disturbed the lush green vegetation. Nets were spread to dry outside cottages, and down on the beach women were collecting seaweed. The tang of brine and seaweed was like iodine, and Minella was near enough to the water to taste salt on her lips. Or was the taste just part of an irrational fear that was taking hold of her? She wished Vasco hadn't brought her here. It was cruel of him to leave her alone at this spot. She was beginning to re-live the horror of that night in the sea so vividly her clothes felt wet and she was shaking, for it was all much worse in retrospect than when she had been only semi-conscious.

She covered her ears to shut out the sound of the sea and tried to look away, but the black-garbed women searching the shore were like carrion crows, and for one gruesome, terrifying minute the bundles they carried took on the form of Greg and Annette.

Slowly Minella rid herself of the vision, focusing on the ribbons of wrack until she could see they were nothing more sinister than seaweed, but she was trembling uncontrollably and the perspiration beaded on her skin felt like drops of ice. Remembering how it had been when she collapsed at Sam's feet, she made a determined effort to shake off this renewed attack of nerves.

'Minella Farmer, you won't gain anything by staging the Victorian vapours here. There's no one to pick her up, for one thing.' She clenched her teeth to stop them chattering. 'And you wouldn't like it if Sam Stafford came along and gave a repeat performance either, so face life the way Greg would expect.'

She allowed herself to sit on a rock, just in case her legs gave way, but scorned any other concession to weakness, and after a few minutes she was warmer and in control of things. But she continued the scolding therapy until a man appeared at the top of the hill. He came towards her, an overweight figure and bushy hair making him instantly recognisable as Dr Henrique Porva. A cherubic smile rounded his cheeks, creased the corners of his eyes and showed strong white teeth beneath a full black moustache. Funny, she had no recollection of the moustache at all, and when he was near she discovered he wasn't even as old as she had thought. His hair was as black as Vasco's.

'Minella Sparrow, I am so pleased to see you! You are better.' He held out his hands, drawing her to her feet.

'How did you know I was here?' she asked, and amazed herself by popping a kiss on each of those olive-skinned cheeks as if he was a long-lost relative.

'Ah, I have spies.'

'Spies?'

'The children. They tell me a foreign lady knocks at my door, so I know it is you. And I see the iron machine that belongs to Vasco.'

She laughed at his description, tension melting away. 'He's taking me to Horta, but we had to stop here first.'

'Does Sam know you trust yourself with that reckless young man?' They had started walking, but he paused, turning to her with a troubled frown.

'It's none of his business,' said Minella.

'Ah, but it is. He has cared much for you.'

Her face coloured at the censure, but Henrique Porva was biased. Sam was his friend.

'He was out when I left,' she told him truthfully. 'And I don't think he'll mind. He doesn't want me there anyway. Like you once said, he doesn't like women.'

'Women in general . . . perhaps,' he agreed, with an eloquent shrug. 'I was hasty when I said that, and I did not expect you to remember.'

They arrived at a gate at the back of his house which he opened, leading her into an overgrown yard where the weeds flowered in spectacular profusion. To Minella it was more beautiful than a carefully cultivated garden.

'Why doesn't Sam like Vasco either?' she asked, trying not to sound too inquisitive. 'They must have been friends at one time for Sam to have taught him such good English.'

The look he gave her was guarded and he didn't answer straight away, but he could see she was anxious.

He said: 'Vasco learned many things from Sam. He was always at his house with Benita and they were close, but one day he stole something very valuable to Sam and he never forgave him. Never, even though it is back now.'

Minella's eyes widened. 'What did he steal?'

Flowers gave way to bins and pots of all sizes near the house, arranged with a collector's precision which stopped it becoming like a tip. Henrique Porva never discarded anything that might come in useful.

'You are . . . how you say . . .?' He tapped his nose, seeking the word he wanted. 'You are a nosey English Miss.'

She just loved Henrique Porva. 'I know I am,' she laughed. 'But I really *do* want to know what it was. A watch? Money?'

'No. It was a painting. But I should not be telling you. Please do not say anything about it. I am fond of Vasco, too.'

Henrique twittered on, unaware of Minella's reaction to the information. She felt as if she had been winded, the breath thumped suddenly out of her, and there was a pain in her stomach. It seemed ages ago that she had been down at the lakeside, peering through the window of Sam's locked hut, yet it was only a few hours. Everything that had happened since stemmed from that moment when she had stumbled on a cache of hidden paintings. So Vasco had found them, too. No wonder Sam was so violently opposed to him, if there was something there he wanted to keep secret. She'd been trying not to think about it, pushing it to the back of her mind until she was far enough removed from Sam to consider the facts objectively. She didn't like him, but it wasn't fair to judge him on a single discovery which might only have seemed suspicious because she was in a feverish, over-sensitive state. But now it became more intriguing.

She was only half listening to Henrique. He had gone on to talk about relative values, how something that meant a lot to one person might mean nothing to another.

'That is why I cannot clear out my store,' he said, opening a door which had once been green but was now so blistered from the sun only flaking strips of paint remained. The house, being built on a slope, had a basement at the back and it was crammed with accumulated objects, the conglomeration in the yard being only an overflow. 'Come, Minella Sparrow, I will show you something special.'

Among the more recent treasures he uncovered a lifebelt, scraps of weed dried on to the framework but its white surface as fresh as if it had been scrubbed. He held it up.

'This is what saved your life, so I keep it,' he said.

Vasco burst in through the door like a tornado, singing in a tenor voice which struck an incongruous note in the quiet of late afternoon and echoed round the

Aladdin's cave. Minella was unaware of him. She was staring at the lifebelt in disbelief, afraid to touch it because the tale it told was too incredible.

'You've made a mistake,' she said. 'This isn't the one.'

'I assure you it is. Vasco will bear me out. This is the lifebelt to which our little bird was clinging, is it not?'

Vasco's song faded away and he took the belt from Henrique to study it. '*Si*, it is the one. All that is left, I think, of the *Nineveh*. I am so sad for you, Minella.'

'But you don't have to be!' Minella gasped. Her heart was beating furiously and she thought she would burst with excitement. 'That's not the name of the yacht I was on. I don't know how I managed to grab hold of *that* lifebelt, but it certainly didn't come from the *Delphine Rose*, which was the name of our yacht.' She gave a cry of joy and flung herself in Henrique's arms. 'Don't you see! If it was the *Nineveh* that broke up then the boat I was on is all right!'

'That is good,' said Vasco.

'Good? It's a miracle!' cried Minella. 'My brother must be alive!'

CHAPTER FIVE

THEY were on the road again, winging towards Horta, and Minella was exultant. She clung to Vasco fearlessly, his reckless driving now thrilling her because she felt lightheaded, and when he burst into song she joined in, though their voices hardly carried above the raucous engine.

It was evening already. The streets of Horta were quiet until they reached an avenue bordering the sea, and a stream of evening visitors drifted aimlessly from one end to the other, or sat under the palms and gazed across at the majestic mountain over the water called Pico, the same as the island which had given it birth. Vasco pottered the length of the Avenida Marginal, past an exotic park draped richly in every shade of green, and down to the Largo do Infante between the sea wall and a yachtsman's paradise of bars and chandlers. He stopped by one of the bars.

'You wait for me here,' he said. 'I will park the motorbike and come back for you.'

Minella gazed around with bright, excited eyes, reborn after days in a grey world of hopelessness, and felt like smiling at everyone. Greg was alive, and she was impatient to find out where he was so that they could be reunited, and just in case he had been directed to Horta she scanned the face of every yachtsman who passed by, though she knew it would be a fairy tale if he appeared. When Vasco returned he would tell her where she could start making enquiries.

The seats outside the bar were packing cases and some boys with a transistor, who had been trying to chat her up in their native Portuguese, made room for her to sit. She thanked them in English and shook her head when they made signs offering to pour some red wine from the jug on the table.

'Cracas?' One of the boys pushed a plateful of scarlet crabs and things that looked like oysters towards her, but at the risk of offending them she refused again with a smile. It was impossible to hold a proper conversation, and she wished Vasco would hurry. They were beginning to get annoying, thinking perhaps she lingered there purposely, and there was no mistaking the gist of their remarks. She was being propositioned.

She got up and walked away, afraid they would follow her, but the wine had made them lazy and they lost interest. She didn't feel safe, though, until she was well clear of the bar, and then she stood in a craft shop doorway to regain her composure.

Where was Vasco? He was supposed to be looking after her, but he had done a disappearing trick and she couldn't rely on anyone. She glanced in the window at a display of local lace and artificial hydrangeas, but after a moment it was her reflection that riveted her attention. She looked awful!—scruffy, hair unkempt after the motorbike ride, shirt and jeans creased and stained. No wonder those boys had taken her for a good-timer! She looked as if a meal wouldn't come amiss and there were dark circles under her eyes, but there was nothing she could do about it. She ran her fingers through her hair because she hadn't a comb. It made no improvement. Vasco had probably been glad to escape, and it could be she had seen the last of him.

In an acute attack of loneliness, bordering on panic, she knew what it felt like to be a down-and-out without money or possessions, not knowing where the next meal or bed for the night was coming from. People passed by, uncaring. But Minella hadn't been on the sidelines when courage was handed out, and she reminded herself that she had always had a spirit of adventure. All the same, she wished Sam was around.

Sam. She pinched herself sharply for being so

ridiculous. It was partly to get away from him that she
had made this dash to Horta, and now she was soft
enough to wish he would appear and make everything
all right. Perhaps it was because he was the only English
person she knew here and he represented a link with
home. There couldn't be any other reason. She tried to
push him out of her mind, but a persistent memory of
being carried up the beach from the sea in strong,
protective arms haunted her like beautiful music. If
only Sam had been as warm-hearted and romantic as
that first impression and not harshly overbearing, she
would have been completely under his spell by now. She
might even have fallen in love with him. Heaven forbid!
What was it about the man that made her crave
information, and now a glimpse of him?

She took another look at her reflection, knew that
Sam, too, would be appalled at the mess she looked,
and decided it was time to do something positive about
her situation. No good waiting around for help.
Tucking her shirt more tidily into her jeans and lifting
her chin with new resolve, she found the nearest
cloakroom where she could start by washing her hands
and face. It would have been lovely to apply some
make-up, but she had to make do with biting her lips to
give them colour. Damp fingers through her hair
achieved a bit more improvement.

Next stop was the tourist office she had seen nearby,
and there she learned that there were five Consular
offices in Horta, none of them British. When she told
her story it was received with obvious scepticism and
she was advised to try either the Passport Control
Office, the police station or the Club Naval da Horta,
though they doubted whether the latter would be able
to do anything. In other words, they thought she was
trying to pull a fast one, suggesting that the police
station was really her best bet. Rather than have the
humiliation of being refused admission to the Club
Naval da Horta, she decided to take their advice.

The police station was about two blocks away. A girl in the tourist office came outside with Minella and pointed out the Matriz church, telling her to head in that direction. When she passed a supermarket on the way she stood at the door and looked longingly inside, like a child with empty pockets glueing its nose to a sweetshop window. There were so many things she wanted to buy.

It was fairly easy to find a policeman who spoke English.

'I want to find out how I can contact my brother quickly,' she said to him. 'He's on a yacht called *Delphine Rose* which was taking part in the Westerly Cup race. I was washed overboard last week in the storm, and there's been such a mix-up.'

'You have your *passaporte*?' the policeman asked, without much interest.

'No, I haven't anything. I told you, I was washed overboard from a yacht.'

He eyed her suspiciously. 'You are here without a *passaporte*, and no money?'

'That's right.'

'It is all very irregular. A . . . tall story.'

'I know how it must sound, but it's true. You must believe me!' Minella was getting het up. 'That's why I've got to find my brother, so that he can come and take me home. You see, we thought he was dead, but now I know he can't be. It was a different yacht. . . .'

'What is your name?' The policeman was making some half-hearted notes.

'Minella Farmer.'

He put down his pen impatiently. 'Why did you not say that first?' he demanded. 'Mr Stafford has already been informed of the messages from Mr Farmer that he is on his way here. Until he arrives Mr Stafford is responsible for you, and I think it better if you stay where he can keep an eye on you. Without a *passaporte* it would not do for you to get into trouble.'

Minella was seething. How dared the man talk to her as if she was a vagrant, policeman or not! He made her so furious she hadn't yet digested the important part of what he'd said.

'If there's news about my brother I want to hear it direct, not have it passed on to me through someone else,' she said, the authoritative tone conflicting with her appearance, making the policeman scrutinise her afresh. 'Perhaps you'll be kind enough to give me the details, as I'm not staying with Mr Stafford any more.'

'Your position here is difficult, Mees Farmer. I understand how you feel, but without Mr Stafford's guarantee of your good conduct it would be even more difficult, and *you* must understand us. We wish to help. Now, if you wait I will telephone the Border Authorities and ask them to repeat the message for you, but I strongly advise you to return to Mr Stafford's custody.'

'Custody? I'm not under age, and I object to having Sam Stafford as some sort of guardian!'

'Wait, please,' he said, his calm voice unchanged, unimpressed, and he sauntered away to another office.

A shaft of light split the gloom, a million dust particles dancing along it as the door opened and disturbed the air. Some yachtsmen came in, and Minella was tempted to approach them in the hope they might be English, but when they spoke together it was in a guttural language she didn't recognise, possibly Scandinavian. They were welcomed with smiles. If the policeman who spoke English had smiled it would have made all the difference. Suddenly she dreaded him coming back, and without questioning the wisdom of the move she darted outside, like one of Fagin's pickpockets waiting for the right moment to escape from the law. It had been claustrophobic in there.

She waited a moment on the pavement, having used evasive tactics for the second time in less than an hour, and wondered what her third predicament would be. It didn't take long to find out.

She was very tired, but an obstinate streak in her cast tiredness aside in the determination to continue her own investigations. She would find the Border authorities, whoever they might be, and find out exactly what was going on.

Elation at having Greg's safety confirmed was tempered now with irritation at the way things had been handled, and as she started retracing her steps to the harbour her mood became progressively worse until she was very angry indeed. And it was Sam who was at the core of that anger. Sam had had word from the Border authorities about Greg, yet he hadn't told her, and she had gone on grieving for her brother when there was no need. How could he possibly be so cruel? Oh, what a detestable man! To think she had been softening towards him only a short time ago, when he was capable of such treachery. Whatever reason could he have had for withholding such wonderful news, knowing how much Greg meant to her? She could only think of one. He had wanted to keep her at the cottage long enough to make her yield, and this morning's brutal kissing had been just the start. She touched her lips experimentally, and set them tingling at the memory. No one had ever kissed her like that before, and the force he had used was an insult, bitterness the only emotion. Well, he hadn't won. It was a good thing she'd had the sense to get away.

'Oh, Greg, thank God you're safe,' she murmured. 'Just hurry up and get me out of this mess!'

So involved were her thoughts she didn't notice she had missed the turning to the harbour and was walking along a road lined on either side with white houses. Past a church on the left with the twin towers and patterns on the white façade in grey lava stone that she had come to recognise. Her feet were dragging with exhaustion and she had no idea where she was heading, so she could hardly believe her eyes when, at the end of the street, she came to a completely different bay with lovely old houses edging close to the sea. A huge moon, red as a watermelon, hung above the rooftops preparing to take off into the darkening sky, and it touched the purple-black sea with fire. This was the old whaling port of Pim, almost enclosed by two volcanic cones, and Minella stood and stared. The two bays had only a ribbon of land between them, threaded with a few dozen houses.

She wandered a little way further, with visions of spending the night on a bench, then she sank down on a bollard to rest and reassess her position. The police knew she was in Horta without money or a *passaporte*, so they wouldn't be too pleased if they found her sleeping rough. She wouldn't like it herself, either, but where was there to go? She hadn't a clue what had happened to Vasco, and didn't relish the thought of trying to trace Sam, even if she knew how to start. *He* seemed to be well known to the police, too, she thought. The policeman had mentioned his name as though he was quite a celebrity, a respected citizen to whom they would entrust a harmless alien without papers, apparently.

Thinking of Sam, she lifted her eyes and glanced idly at the nearest houses. One of them, large and attractive, appeared to be a studio with the front window extended to display size, and as she looked the door beside it opened, producing a golden oblong of light in the semi-darkness. Two people came out. Minella darted to the shadows, intuition warning her that this was about to become predicament number three. She was right. The girl in the doorway was an elegant brunette with long hair and a tall, graceful figure. The man, on whom she bestowed an infatuated smile, was Sam.

Minella's heart tilted, capered erratically, then righted itself. He didn't return the smile, or seem aware of its content which had been obvious even at a distance, but the girl took his arm and Minella blinked hard to try and dispel the scene. Sam's hard, muscular arm crooked to accommodate the possessive hand, and the unwilling spectator in the shadows felt strangely sick. For someone who didn't like women, Sam Stafford exuded a strong magnetism, attracting them without any effort, and Minella remembered how quickly she had felt the lure of it herself.

They were coming towards her and she flattened herself against the wall. He was talking to the girl in Portuguese, but his voice had the same low, seductive ring calculated to set the spine tingling and blood racing through the veins. Oh, he was a master of philandering! She wished she knew what he was saying, then was glad she didn't. Inexplicable tears stung her eyes and she would have given anything to be beautiful like the Azorean girl. Sam's car was parked at the end of the road and he opened the door for her, then got in himself and drove off.

Minella came back into the light, her temples throbbing and a pain in her heart she had never experienced before as she stared after the departing car in forlorn confusion. Part of her wanted to make a rude sign with her fingers, but the sigh that escaped her was pure despair at not being able to fathom the true direction of her feelings.

She was sitting on the bollard again when a motor-bike buzzed round the corner like an angry hornet attacking her eardrums. She covered her ears with her hands as Vasco screeched to a stop beside her, exhaust fumes belching into the soft air which a few minutes previously had retained the girl's heady perfume.

'Where have you been?' Vasco demanded. 'I ask you to wait and when I look for you you are not there. Why?' His handsome young face was clouded with annoyance.

'I *did* wait,' said Minella, and she told him what had happened, matching his temper because she was in no mood to make allowances. She was relieved to see him, but that didn't make his long disappearance excusable.

'You didn't even buy me a drink, and I'd no money to buy one,' she finished. 'It made me feel ridiculous.'

He was contrite. 'I am sorry—I did not think. I was in a hurry to get something important and it was more difficult than I think, but I have it now.' He gave a triumphant grin which dispelled the frown. 'Also I have brought wine, to make up for my mistake. Come, we have only a little way to go and then everything will be all right.'

Minella clambered back on the motorbike, trying not to think of Sam's girl-friend stepping elegantly into his car, and she giggled. Vasco was fun, which was more than could be said of Sam, and if she was taking bets on who was likely to spend the happiest evening she knew which way she would gamble. She rested her cheek against Vasco's back and juddered along with her eyes closed, uncaring where he planned to take her because anywhere was better than having no place to go. Or so she thought, in that moment of temporary respite.

Vasco slowed down and turned right, off the road. The surface was now uneven and the jarring so unpleasant she sat up straight and looked around. They were driving round the harbour, perilously near the edge of the quay, and he took no notice of fishermen who shook fists at him as he bounced over the cobbles, just laughed in high humour. Further along, the harbour arm stretched protectively across the bay and he continued on to where yachts were tied. There was a feeling of unreality about the caper, heightened by the sight of strange paintings on the wall appearing bright and almost frightening in the headlight. He pulled up beside a large power cruiser and dismounted.

'You see,' said Vasco proudly, 'I had to get permission before I could use the boat, and I could not find my friend, but it is all right.'

Minella looked at the boat, and back to Vasco. 'You mean we're going on board?'

Minella worked for a company near Brighton who made dinghies, but she also knew a lot about the expensive side of the trade and recognised the worth of the cruiser, which was all of thirty-two feet long. Vasco certainly had wealthy friends. It was a beautiful boat.

Vasco stepped on board and uncovered the hatch, but she didn't follow. There were nervous butterflies playing havoc with her inside and she clasped her hands together tightly when he stretched out one of his to help her.

'I don't think we should, Vasco. I've got a funny feeling. . . .'

'You do not trust me?' he asked, offended.

'Of course I do, but . . . this place . . . it doesn't seem right.' She glanced at the wall where the moon shone on the painted stones, and all the yacht owners who had decorated them over the years seemed to be warning her not to fall in with the smiling boy. Vasco was a rogue. He was inviting her aboard a borrowed boat, the bag he had taken from the panier of his bike clanking with bottles, and only a fool would misjudge his intentions. Hadn't she flown from Sam Stafford because he had tried to take advantage, and yet here she was inviting trouble. She hung back.

'Minella Sparrow, I will not hurt you,' he laughed. His tone was light and he was making fun of her hesitation. 'What harm is there in cooking a meal and eating it in comfort? Much better than a bar. Then we can talk a little before I go home. You had nowhere to stay the night, so I . . . magic it for you because I am clever, but I promise I will not touch you, only to help you now.'

'I've climbed on board enough boats not to need any help,' she said, indignantly. 'Did you say you've got food?' She suddenly realised how hungry she was, and convinced herself the butterflies in her stomach were no more than hunger pangs.

'Bread and fishes,' he smiled, holding up the bag.

'Well, if we're feeding the five thousand I suppose there's safety in numbers.'

'What is that?' he asked, puzzled.

'Just a joke,' said Minella, and climbed aboard.

Vasco lit the lamps and took the food up to the galley, emptying the bag with a flourish while Minella watched.

'I'll do the cooking if you like,' she volunteered timidly. 'My sister-in-law did it on the *Delphine Rose*, but I'm quite capable.'

'I will do it. You find the plates.' Vasco produced a pan from a cupboard, and soon the smell of mackerel frying was so strong they had to open the hatch. Minella was ravenous, and the sight of the fish with flat bread cakes and goat's milk butter looked as good as a banquet.

'I thought you did not like Sam Stafford,' said Vasco, filling two tall glasses with wine.

'I don't.'

'But you were waiting for him just now. I nearly did not stop.'

'Whatever do you mean?' she asked.

He put two plates of mackerel on the narrow table, sat beside her and lifted his glass in a toast, to which she responded absentmindedly.

'Vasco, what do you mean?' she persisted.

He ignored the question and started eating, and after a second Minella did the same. The fish was delicious, the wine equally so, and she had consumed a fair amount of each before Vasco went back to the subject.

'You were sitting outside his studio,' he said.

Minella choked and put down her fork. 'Sam's studio?' she spluttered. 'What does he do there?'

'He sells the pictures that he paints, of course. You did not know he is an artist?' He looked at her strangely and when she shook her head he went on: 'In Horta he is famous. All the tourists buy his paintings because they are pictures of Fayal.'

So the explanation to the secret hut was as simple as that. She laughed. It hadn't crossed her mind that Sam might produce works of art himself. There wasn't a sign of any at the cottage.

'So he must keep some of his paintings down by the lake, then,' she said, half to herself.

Vasco's eyes narrowed and he paused. 'You know about those?'

'Not really, except that I went down to the hut and looked through the window, and Sam was very cross.' Vasco poured more wine in her glass. She giggled and gave a little hiccough. 'Isn't it silly, I really thought they were old masters he'd stolen and stashed away. It was such a perfect hiding place. Serves me right for having such a vivid imagination!'

He threw back his head and laughed. 'That is *very* funny.' He finished eating and pushed aside his plate, then leaned closer to her. 'In a way you are right, though. There are pictures in that hut he does not wish anyone to see.'

'Really?' Her eyes widened and she cupped her chin with her hands, gazing at him in fascination. At last she was beginning to learn something about Sam. 'Tell me,' she begged.

'In a little while,' he promised. 'First we must drink some *aguardente*. Finish your wine.'

She obediently drained her glass and popped the last piece of bread in her mouth. It had been a fabulous meal, but she was glad she hadn't any more fish to eat, because the plate was becoming hazy and she wouldn't have been able to concentrate on finding bones. In fact she began to wonder whether the sea was getting rough, because nothing in the cabin seemed quite steady. She gave another little hiccough.

'I—don't think I want any more to drink,' she said, when Vasco brought another bottle over.

'Ah, but no meal is over until you have had a little *aguardente*. If you do not try it I shall be offended.' He poured some in her glass, then his own.

She took a sip of the fiery liquid and wrinkled her nose. It burned her throat. 'It's very strong,' she said. 'What is it?'

'Brandy. We distil it from our grapes at home.'

'Oh! Isn't that illegal?' She tried to be severe, but couldn't compose her features, and another giggle escaped. 'You really are quite wicked, Vasco.'

'Why? Everyone makes brandy if they grow grapes and medlars, so why am I wicked?'

'You're trying to get me drunk, but I'm not going to have any more.' She put the glass away from her, but he covered her hand with his own and guided it back.

'It will do you good. Already you have colour in your cheeks.' He leaned over and dropped a kiss on the bright spots of colour, and she jerked her head aside. 'You know I will never harm you.'

'Then don't you think it's time you were going? I'm sure your friend who kindly said I could sleep on the boat wouldn't approve of *you* staying late.'

'No,' said Vasco, 'he would not approve at all. So we will wash the plates.'

Minella breathed a sigh of relief as he took the plates to the stainless steel sink and soaked then in some water. She would have helped him, but her legs were so wobbly she felt quite weak and she stayed where she was on the turquoise upholstered berth, wishing everything wasn't so hazy.

'You promised to tell me about the paintings in the hut,' she said.

Vasco smiled. 'You are impatient. I think it is because you are attracted to Sam, just like all the women.'

'I am *not!*'

'Yet when I say his name you come alive. I wish you would look at me that way.' A discontented shadow crossed his face. 'It is not any use, you know. He only plays with women. It amuses him. Me, I love them all, but they do not look at me the way they do him. It is not fair.'

He was right. She had first-hand experience of his diversions, but it wouldn't do for Vasco to know. She laughed. 'I'm sure you have dozens of girl-friends.'

'I have. The girls chase me,' he boasted, 'but they are not like Sam's girls. His are always ... special. I cannot explain.'

'Classy,' she suggested.

'What is that?'

'Well. . . .' She paused thoughtfully. Then: 'Like models, perhaps.'

'*Si!* Like girls in magazines.'

She took another sip of brandy after all, feeling oddly depressed. 'So that counts me out.'

She turned away, but Vasco had seen her expression and the shadow darkened.

'I knew you liked him better than me,' he said, slipping back to the bunk with feline grace which disconcerted her even before his next words. 'But he cannot have you. I will make you like me best and then you will not want to look at Sam again.'

'You're jealous,' she accused, pressing herself further into the corner.

'Yes, I am jealous. And I hate Sam Stafford.'

He wasn't smiling any more, and the Latin eyes burned into her. The cabin was not very big and the change of mood hung heavily in the claustrophobic atmosphere. There was no air and it was very hot.

'Is that why you stole one of his paintings?'

It was a cruel question, like hitting below the belt, but it had the right effect. He straightened up angrily and his eyes hooded with resentment.

'What do you know about that?' he asked. He became guarded, and Minella knew it had been wrong to mention it.

'I'm sorry,' she apologised. 'It's none of my business, is it?'

She lifted her head and saw a scarf of moonlight draped across the dark water, and the lights of Horta on the other side of the harbour looked a long way away.

'How was I to know she was the girl he was going to marry?' he demanded, incomprehensibly. 'She was so beautiful. I saw the picture many times, and when he put it in the hut with the others I thought he would not mind if I borrowed it. I wanted to look at it every night. I dreamed about her, but I thought she was ... what you say just now ... a model. Ah, if I could meet a girl like that!'

He sighed, his thoughts transparent, and Minella was embarrassed. He had a vivid imagination and he rubbed perspiring hands on his thighs, his shoulders tense. A prickling fear made her edgy and she wished she had listened to the inner voice that had warned her to be cautious. She had been too trusting. Vasco Hernandez was as much a stranger as Sam, and she had already run from one awkward situation.

'I really think you ought to be going now, Vasco,' she said lightly.

He snapped back to the present, his wiry body twisting towards her. She had moved along, hoping to alter the pattern so that he was not between her and the hatch, but when he made no further advance and a boyish grin spread suddenly from his mouth to his eyes, she knew instinctively that there was no need to be afraid.

He drew her to her feet. 'You are not ... classy, but you are beautiful. If I had you I would not need pictures. Thank you for not laughing at me.'

'Why would I do that?'

'Because I fall in love with a painting.' He paused, looking down at her, and black lashes almost hid the dark eyes, though not the diffidence that lurked behind them. He was not really the practised Romeo he would have liked her to believe. 'You see, I talk too much and say wicked things, but I do not have the courage to follow them up. Englishmen, I think, say very little, but they *do* have the courage, and that is why Sam has beautiful women.'

'Oh, Vasco,' she laughed, 'what a thing to say!'

'But it is true. I do not want to leave you, but it is better. It will make you happy, so I say goodnight.'

He gave a rueful smile, and after only a slight hesitation Minella threw her arms round his neck as she might have done if he had been her brother.

'You've been so kind to me,' she said. 'I don't know what I'd have done without you. Thank you for everything.'

And she kissed him warmly, with real gratitude.

Neither of them had heard a sound outside. When the hatch opened they sprang apart and turned simultaneously. In the split second before recognition dawned Vasco received a blow to the chin that sent him reeling backwards, and Minella screamed. The intruder was Sam. He dominated the scene immediately, his tall figure seeming to fill the saloon, and the power of his anger was a tempest bursting in.

'I warned you never to touch Minella!' he raged.

'What right have you got to push your way in here?' Minella demanded.

As she spoke the full impact of his temper shifted in her direction. Unable to meet the fury in his steely blue eyes, her own flicked upwards and she saw something she had missed before. Above the hatch was the name of the boat in black and gold letters, *M.V. Samanne*, and the significance struck her as forcibly as the blow to Vasco's chin.

'I have *every* right,' Sam was saying, 'as the boat is mine, and I'm damned if I'll let it be used for illicit lovemaking! Get off, Vasco, and don't ever trick your way on board again!'

Vasco was nursing his chin, too stunned to be coherent.

'Stop shouting at him!' cried Minella. 'He did it for me because I hadn't anywhere to sleep. . . .'

'So the pair of you were going to sleep here. Cosy! Pity for your sake my friend with the keys has a suspicious mind and checked with me that Vasco had my permission to use them. Get going, Vasco, before I *really* lose my temper.'

'He was just going anyway!' she yelled.

'Get!' roared Sam. He caught Vasco's collar and propelled him towards the hatch, shoving him out on to the deck. 'For two pins I'd make you take this little tramp with you, but for my sins I've been made responsible for her!'

Minella struck him with all the strength she could muster, catching his cheek with the flat of her hand, and success lay in the equal unexpectedness of her retaliation. His head jerked sideways, but failed to avoid the attack.

'My God, Sam Stafford, how I hate you!' she said, her voice coldly quiet now and filled with enmity.

CHAPTER SIX

MINELLA awoke the next morning in a luxurious bed with brass rails at the head and foot, a duvet in fine white cotton with almond-blossom patterns loosely over her. The heavy coral curtains which had been drawn the night before were now pulled back to reveal a balcony edged with white wrought iron, and golden sunlight intensified the golden shine on floorboards covered only with two Indian dhurries. It was a beautiful room. A rich mahogany chest of drawers was the only piece of furniture, but there was also an antique wash-stand with a jug and basin. Steam was coming from the jug and she realised it was full of hot water for her to wash. There wasn't a sound anywhere.

Sam had brought her to the room last night. It was on the first floor of the house where he had his studio, but she had been too tired to care where it was as long as there was a bed where she could sleep. She pushed aside the duvet and stretched, catlike, refreshed by the long, undisturbed hours of rest, and wondered who had come in with the water. There was no clock for her to know what time it was, but the sun was not very high, so she permitted herself a few more minutes with her head on the fragrant white pillow.

The events of last night were hazy. She remembered how angry she had been when Sam struck Vasco. She had thought Vasco would put up a fight, but the sound of his motorbike had rapidly faded as he escaped round the harbour arm, and she was left with Sam, infuriated by his interference. So he owned the boat, but that didn't excuse him for the way he behaved. She had gone to the hatch, determined to flounce away and leave him, but something strange had happened when she got out

90

in the air. Her head went woolly and she seemed to be spinning in dizzy circles.

'I might have known he'd get you drunk first,' she heard Sam say, as he caught her before she toppled into the water. 'He wouldn't have the guts otherwise!'

It didn't seem worth defending Vasco any more, even if she'd been capable, and she put up no resistance when Sam carried her to his car and dumped her unceremoniously in the seat where he had handed the elegant brunette earlier. Half asleep, Minella had staggered up a flight of steps behind the studio, his fingers gripping her wrist as if she was likely to run away, and when he opened the bedroom door she was too muddled to question his intentions. All she could remember was standing unsteadily on one of the dhurries and looking about her in fascination.

'So this is the place *you* use for illicit love,' she said, and waited for him to close the door. Which he did.

'Sam?'

The wine and *aguardente* had created a mood of blissful abandon where everything was like a dream and she floated on a cloud of contentment. A burning sensation curled upwards from her toes, lighting tiny flames of desire which needed only Sam's touch to blaze with fierce intensity. She held out her arms, and when nothing happened she groaned and rubbed her eyes, trying to clear her blurred vision. She was alone in the room. When Sam closed the door he had gone out and left her.

Remembering the way she had felt, Minella groaned again, this time with shame, and buried her head in the pillow. She had never behaved so disgracefully in her life, and the only consolation was that Sam had not stayed to witness it, and had not taken advantage. She might easily have woken up this morning and found him next to her in bed, and that would have been disaster.

She couldn't understand herself. How could she

possibly have degraded herself like that, allowing a purely physical urge to outweigh all her finer principles? She disliked the man so much and had told him so vehemently, yet a few minutes later she craved for the feel of him near her. It didn't make sense. He was arrogant, insensitive and tyrannical. The way he had felled poor Vasco without provocation was quite inexcusable. She twisted her head out of the suffocating pillow and lay on her back, gazing at the ceiling, and an irrepressible smile came bubbling to the surface. In retrospect it was really quite funny. Imagine being at the centre of a punch-up! Greg would find it hilarious when she told him.

She scrambled out of bed, remembering that this was the day she might be reunited with her brother. The water was cool when she poured it in the basin, but it was lovely to wash properly and she hated putting on the old jeans and shirt once more. Fortunately there was a brush, and she parted her silky brown hair in the middle, leaving only a wisp of bangs over her forehead. Her eyes were wide and shining.

Not sure what to do next, she opened the French windows and went out on to the balcony. Warm, humid air met her and she looked down at a courtyard garden where broad-leafed creepers twined in profusion round trelliswork and an abundance of passionflowers were starred with fragrant, intruding stephanotis. A fig-tree touched the window with the lobes of its thick leaves, as if warning her that all was not as tranquil as it seemed, and a second later Sam appeared.

She was charged with a strange excitement, whipped up by the memory of last night's encounter, but quelled it immediately. Nothing had altered. It was just unfortunate that his particular brand of animal magnetism struck an answering chord in her sometimes, but she would use all her will-power to resist it.

She watched him a moment without detection. His dark hair curled untamed, and a red shirt tucked loosely into tight black cords gave him the look of a buccaneer. She could picture him in the bows of a square-rigged ship, legs astride, cutlass at the ready as his men crouched behind him waiting for the order to board a vessel he had forced to hove to. Had he been Azorean born she would have thought he was descended from the pirates who had raided these shores, for he was a man of the sea and ought to have been born in a swashbuckling age. She was not surprised he owned a powerboat. It went with his image much better than the cottage by the lake.

She was just wondering whether he also owned the house when he turned and caught sight of her, and she was unprepared for the impact of an unsmiling glare. Her heart somersaulted.

'You'd better come down from there,' he called. 'It used to be the custom in these islands for men to start up a courtship with young girls on balconies. You'll find coffee and breakfast downstairs in the kitchen.'

'Thanks—I'm starving!'

Her bedroom, she found, had been directly above the dining room. She came to it via the kitchen just as he was coming in from the courtyard through glass doors. The table was covered with a white cloth inset with handmade lace, and a woman in black brought a fresh pot of coffee, chattering to Sam in Portuguese as she set it down near a basket of crisp rolls.

'Help yourself,' Sam invited, drawing out a cane chair for Minella. 'I had mine earlier.'

'Oh, please, stay and have some more coffee.' She didn't fancy eating alone. The housekeeper, or whoever she was, had already looked down her nose at her as if she was some waif he had brought in. Well, who could blame her? 'There's so much I want to ask you ... like when is Greg coming?'

After a moment Sam condescended to sit opposite, and poured himself some coffee. His unapproachable expression made her livid. She'd begun with a polite question as she was a guest in his house, but he had a lot more to answer for. When he delayed she prepared to do battle.

'*You* knew my brother was alive yesterday morning, yet you didn't tell me. I just don't know how you could be so cruel! They told me at the police station that the Border Authorities had given you a message.'

He ran his fingers through his hair. 'Sparrow, in the few days since you entered my life nothing has gone smoothly. You're the most exasperating creature I've ever met! You're impetuous, inquisitive, delinquent, and . . .' He stopped, biting back the words which would have followed, and those brilliant eyes softened. 'I've nursed you through shock and grief over your brother without having any definite information to go on, and I knew you had to have the facts, one way or the other. I was *not* given any messages from anyone. I drove into Horta because I wasn't satisfied with the inquiries that had been made. I'm not used to apathetic handling of official business, and I put some calls through to London. The first thing I discovered was that you weren't even on the crew list of the *Nineveh*.'

'Because I wasn't on the *Nineveh*. You just assumed that.'

'So I found out. It must have broken up before you fell from the *Delphine Rose*, and by some miracle you came in contact with the lifebelt. I then discovered that the *Delphine Rose* had put back to England because everyone was too upset to carry on with the race, naturally, and a certain Greg Farmer had declared he would never give up searching for you. He'd made enquiries as far as Sâo Miguel. I finally managed to contact him and he said he would catch the first available flight to Lisbon. He should arrive here at about midday.'

Tears of relief welled up unbidden, but she dashed them away. 'Why couldn't you have let me know sooner?'

'Because, my dear Minella, I drove straight back to the cottage, only to find you had cleared off in search of the objectionable Vasco Hernandez.'

'He's *not* objectionable. . . .'

'I followed you to the farm and his brother told me you'd left for Horta on the back of his motorbike. So I washed my hands of you.'

'And found consolation with your girl-friend. I saw you come out of here together.'

Those penetrating eyes focused on her sharply and seemed to see more of her than she liked, then a flicker of humour reached them. 'Do I detect curiosity getting the better of you again?'

'Of course not,' she said.

'Jealousy, then. I can't recall asking what you and Vasco were doing, or were about to do on my boat, so I hardly think my friendship with Consuelo is anything to do with you.'

'Jealous?' gasped Minella. 'Only *you* could be vain enough to presume such a thing. I am *not* jealous! I can't stand you!'

He grinned. 'Methinks your protestations are too strong, Sparrow.'

'And what's that supposed to mean?'

'Think about it. I remember kissing you, and I had the impression you could get to like it.'

Her cheeks flamed and she stood up so suddenly the chair tipped over. As she rushed from the room the woman in black appeared in the kitchen doorway with a tray, which she dropped with a clatter as Minella careered into her.

'Minella!' thundered Sam.

She was murmuring apologies to the woman and picking up broken crockery. When she looked up he was standing over her, a menacing giant with brows like a storm cloud.

'I'm so sorry . . .' she muttered.

He helped her to her feet, but she snatched her hand

away from his as if she had touched live electricity.

'For goodness sake stop behaving like a juvenile!' he snapped. Then seeing the way she rubbed her fingers, he asked anxiously: 'You're not hurt, are you?'

'No. No, I'm not hurt.'

'Good. Then meet me in the studio in ten minutes. We've time to get new clothes for you before we go to the airport.'

'But I haven't any money.'

'I'm sure we can come to some arrangement,' said Sam.

Feeling rather awkward, Minella was waiting in the studio long before ten minutes were up, and she looked around with interest. She found it was called the Stafford Gallery, and the paintings on display were signed simply 'Stafford'. On closer inspection she didn't think much of them. They were impressions of local landmarks, distinctive but not to her taste, and she recognised one as being similar to the painting in the cottage bedroom which had baffled her at first. It was of a tropical Azorean stand with corn cobs hanging to dry like vast hands of bananas such as she had seen in many fields since. The better ones were flower studies of canna lilies, white callas, azaleas and the inevitable hydrangeas. But there were no portraits.

'What do you think of them?' Sam asked, bringing in another to prop on a vacant easel. 'It's been known for demand to outstrip supply.'

She looked at him sharply, trying to establish how serious he was, but his face remained enigmatic. She answered evasively.

'Have you always been an artist?'

'Surely you mean was I *ever* an artist,' he said, and turned to her with a glint of humour. 'I assure you these are merely a commercial venture. It still amazes me when they sell.'

'So what did you do before?' she then ventured to ask.

'Ah,' said Sam, 'would you believe me if I told you

What made Marge burn the toast and miss her favorite soap opera?

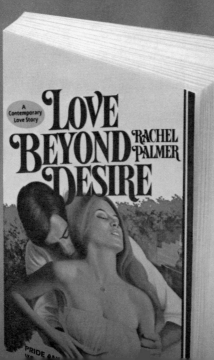

A Contemporary Love Story

LOVE BEYOND DESIRE

RACHEL PALMER

...At his touch, her body felt a familiar wild stirring, but she struggled to resist it. This is not love, she thought bitterly.

PRIDE

A compelling love story of mystery and intrigue... conflicts and jealousies... and a forbidden love that threatens to shatter the lives of all involved with the aristocratic Lopez family.

← Mail this card today for your FREE gifts.

TAKE THIS BOOK
AND TOTE BAG FREE!

Mail to: **SUPERROMANCE**
2504 W. Southern Avenue, Tempe, Arizona 85282

YES, please send me FREE and without any obligation, my SUPERROMANCE novel, *Love Beyond Desire*. If you do not hear from me after I have examined my FREE book, please send me the 4 new SUPERROMANCE books every month as soon as they come off the press. I understand that I will be billed only $2.50 per book (total $10.00). There are no shipping and handling or any other hidden charges. There is no minimum number of books that I have to purchase. In fact, I may cancel this arrangement at any time. *Love Beyond Desire* and the tote bag are mine to keep as FREE gifts even if I do not buy any additional books.

134-CIS-KAE7

Name	(Please Print)	
Address		Apt. No.
City		
State		Zip

Signature   (If under 18, parent or guardian must sign.)

SUPERROMANCE ™

I was drummed out of Military Intelligence?'

She laughed, as he had intended she should. 'You mean MI5!' She was almost gullible enough to accept it, but his mouth quirked into a droll smile which proved he was teasing. And before she could enlarge on the subject the door opened and the girl he had called Consuelo minced in.

In daylight she didn't quite match up to last night's impression. She was older than she had appeared, her olive skin stretched tightly over good bone structure, but fine lines had begun to show and her black hair was too severely styled. Her clothes needed pressing. She spared Minella a cursory glance and went straight to Sam, who greeted her with friendly politeness.

'Sparrow, this is Consuelo, who doesn't speak English,' he said. 'She runs the studio for me, and now she's come we'll go and do our shopping.'

Minella looked from Sam to the girl and back again, and another gurgle of laughter escaped her, though she tried to disguise it as a cough when Consuelo glared. Okay, so she worked here. A curious fluttering, which had started up inside her the moment she appeared, gradually subsided.

To her surprise Sam insisted on shopping with her. When she would have bought a new pair of serviceable jeans and a pair of shorts he made his objections so clear the assistant looked half afraid.

'You are to buy something feminine,' he said, the words delivered slowly for emphasis. 'Otherwise I shall make you put a belt round that old nightdress of Benita's.'

'You will do no such thing! And I haven't much money to spare for clothes anyway, so I shall buy what's most useful.'

'Just now you said you hadn't any money at all,' said Sam. 'So as I'm footing the bill you'll choose something becoming.'

Minella was relieved the girls serving didn't understand. He was being thoroughly unpleasant, and the tone of his voice was enough for her to receive pitying looks. They must have wondered what right he had to be so adamant. She even wondered herself, but decided not to argue any more.

In the end she came out of the shop with a white linen skirt and sleeveless blouse in delphinium blue with frills at the neck, the shorts, a floral skirt in shades of green and a T-shirt embroidered with gold thread. A lovely white silk scarf and strappy sandals completed the new wardrobe, with a pair of flat leather mules thrown in for good measure.

'One more stop,' said Sam, who had waited outside while she bought underwear, 'then back to the house and you can change.'

He took her to a place where a woman was making the most beautiful jewellery from slivers of a whale's tooth, delicate as ivory and finely etched with intricate designs. He picked up a pendant on a gold chain, the most expensive thing, on a bed of velvet used for display. It was so lovely Minella caught her breath when sunlight made it shimmer with magical iridescence.

'It's just beautiful!' she breathed.

'Too good for that scruffy little neck of yours,' he said, handing it back to the woman.

Smarting at the unnecessary affront, Minella turned and walked away, confused and mortified. Trust him to make it seem as if she had been expecting one as a gift! What had he taken her there for anyway? She marched ahead of him, half inclined to thrust the parcels into his arms and refuse them on principle, even though she intended to reimburse him fully at the first opportunity, but an obstinate streak made her decide to keep them. She would show Sam Stafford how wrong he was. She was not some urchin to be patronised. When he saw the real Minella he'd feel ashamed he hadn't volunteered to carry the parcels for her!

Half an hour later she came slowly downstairs to

where he waited, and wasn't disappointed with the reception. The blue of her blouse set off the tan she had acquired earlier in Brighton, and the minimum of make-up was needed, mostly to emphasise her eyes which glowed beneath the soft brown bangs. A straight skirt and high-heeled sandals made her seem taller, and she walked with an awareness that her legs and figure were good and shown to advantage. Sam's eyes rested on her with undisguised appreciation, but he didn't comment on the transformation. His gaze travelled upwards from her toes and stopped to focus on the full, gentle mouth with lips slightly parted in wonder. She hadn't expected the moment of revelation to be so important to her, but as she watched admiration softening his angular face a throbbing sensation weakened her limbs and pounded in her temples, and she realised that his opinion of her mattered quite a lot.

'You may have changed your plumage, but I shall still call you Sparrow,' he said, drawing her towards him. 'I'm sorry I offended you. I was teasing you cruelly because I didn't want to give you this until you'd emerged from your chrysalis.'

The pendant gleamed as he let it fall against her smooth throat and he fastened it. When his fingers played against the sensitive hollow at the nape of her neck Minella experienced an ecstasy so intense it seemed there could be no greater rapture, and she was afraid to look up in case he should see her agitation.

'I don't want it,' she protested, trying to move away. Being so close to him disturbed her even more, and that treacherous physical attraction she had thought was permanently quenched became a renewed danger.

'It was meant for you, Sparrow. Please accept it.'

She hesitated. He sounded genuinely anxious and she couldn't detect any condescending undercurrent. She let her fingers slide over the pendant now nestling between the frills of her blouse and knew she would treasure it all her life.

Standing on tiptoe, she brushed his cheek with the lightest kiss.

'Thank you, Sam.'

A surge of happiness swept through her. She and Sam had called a truce and it was a relief to know she wouldn't have to be continually on the defensive when they met Greg in less than an hour. Greg would get on well with Sam. In many ways they were alike, stubborn and strong-willed, and annoyingly chauvinistic at times, but both had great charm when they chose to use it. Recognising these like traits, she was surprised she didn't like Sam better. Maybe she would from now on. She couldn't wait for them to all be together.

But as it turned out she had to wait quite a lot longer. When she and Sam arrived at the white airport building it was to be told that a dispute at São Miguel involving traffic controllers had delayed the midday flight for at least five hours. Minella hid her disappointment well, but Sam was not deceived, and he gave her shoulder a sympathetic squeeze before taking her back to Horta.

'It's no good sitting around wasting time,' he said, 'so I suggest we make the most of the day and take a spin in the *Samanne*. How about it?'

'Surely you've got more important things to do,' said Minella, tentatively. Much as she would love a trip on the powerboat she hadn't forgotten the scene on board last night and guessed the remnants of the mackerel supper would be still around to cause friction. But he was insistent, and in spite of her opposition she found herself in the cockpit with him a little while later as they cruised out of the harbour. The strange thing was the saloon showed no sign at all of recent use. Sam had taken care of it the same as he did everything else, and she didn't question him.

When she looked back at Horta it seemed to rise out of the ocean and hug the hillsides like an elegant adornment. Picturesque houses lined the seafront, merging with the walls of the old fortress of Santa Cruz, and splashes of colour blazed from parks and gardens. It was easy to see why it had been a favourite port of call in the days of sailing ships.

'Are all the islands as beautiful as Fayal?' she asked, as he opened up the throttle and headed out to sea before turning westwards.

'In their different ways,' he said. 'Each one has its own characteristics.'

'And there are nine of them.'

'That's right. But did you know that for a few weeks there were ten? I'm taking you to see where the tenth one appeared before sinking back into the sea.'

Keeping the coastline to starboard, the *Samanne* lifted her bows clear of the water and sped towards the north of the island, white foam fanning out in their wake. It was exhilarating to feel the wind tearing through her hair and spray like fine rain on her face, cool and wholesome. Both of them had hurriedly changed into shorts and T-shirts, and she hadn't had time to feel nervous about going out in a boat for the first time since she had been rescued.

Sam knew endless stories about Fayal and entertained her with them as they travelled, shouting to make himself heard above the roar of the engine. He told her about Jos van Hurtere whose wife, Brites, had been a lady-in-waiting at the Portuguese court. Her husband had heard the island had mountains of solid silver, but she had only nightmares of sailing to an island abounding in wild beasts, so when she set foot on Fayal and found it a paradise of flowers she was so overjoyed she had a church built as a thanksgiving. And their son-in-law became one of Fayal's most famous inhabitants. He was Martin of Bohemia, who created the Nuremberg globe. In 1597 Fayal was sacked by Sir Walter Raleigh during the Spanish occupation, and Captain Cook once stayed in Horta to check his instruments. Minella was fascinated. Sam's love of the island was infectious and she found herself scanning the coastline eagerly, as if a caravel from the Orient might be sheltering there. The pictures he painted in words were more vivid than his brush-strokes on canvas.

Presently he cut the speed and turned towards land. They cruised quietly round a headland and dropped anchor in dark waters beneath forbidding cliffs, and the scenery was some of the most desolate she had ever seen. It was a cross between a lunar landscape and slagheaps surrounding ancient collieries. The sand on the deserted beach was black, particles of it reaching them like a miniature dust-storm, and no plants grew.

'This is Capelinhos,' said Sam. 'You see that tower way over to the right? That was once the lighthouse, and now it's so far inland it can't be used.'

'How did it happen?' asked Minella, gazing in awe. 'Was it the eruption you told me about?'

'That was the one. When the island disappeared again what was left of it became an extension of Fayal.'

She shuddered. 'It feels eerie, as if the sun has gone.'

And as she spoke a mist started rolling in from the north, giving the place an even more mysterious atmosphere.

'I walk out this way sometimes,' he told her, 'when I'm feeling jaded and at odds with the world. It's a primeval sort of place that helps me put my insignificant troubles in the right perspective. I suppose I'm a fatalist at heart.'

He looked into the distance with eyes trained to see more than surface detail, and pain she couldn't begin to comprehend communicated itself to her through the timbre of his voice. She wanted to ask him questions, but they would be too personal and she didn't have the courage. With the mist it became cooler and goose pimples covered her arms. She shivered, and Sam laughed, throwing back his head to let the deep-throated sound roll out and dispel the spirits of Capelinhos. Then he weighed anchor and started the engine.

'Okay, Sparrow, let's head back to the sun.'

They swept round in an arc and his hands steering the course back to Horta were supremely capable. It had been a strange sojourn, yet in that short time he had revealed a great deal about himself. Compassion stirred in her because this giant of a man, who had seemed invincible, had allowed her to glimpse the vulnerable core that sought reassurance and needed to identify with fundamental things. She had once wondered if he was lonely. Now she *knew* that he was.

He dropped anchor again quite close to the town, along a stretch of coast which he called Laginha. Minella could hardly believe only a short distance separated the two places, for here was a sun-drenched vista of rock formation with a road running above it edged with tamarisks.

'This is lovely,' she breathed. 'I feel as if I've escaped from something I didn't understand.'

'There's an unpredictable feel about Capelinhos,' he agreed. 'Yet it's a great tourist attraction.' He took hold of her hand and smiled. 'Let's forget about it and enjoy the sun. I wish I hadn't taken you there.'

They went up to the bows where they could sunbathe on the warm deck and Minella lay on her stomach with her hands cupping her chin. She stared dreamily at the dazzling ocean, her thoughts of the hours she had spent in the water, and wondered how far she had drifted on the current which had brought her to these shores. Her rescue seemed more miraculous than ever when the smallness of the islands was taken into account.

She turned to speak of it to Sam, but he had stripped off his shirt and was lying on his back with his hands above his head, his eyes closed against the sun, and she was arrested by his strength even in repose. For the first time she could study him undetected. His tanned skin gleamed and dark hair curled from his throat to the top of his shorts. Powerful limbs were as brown as the shiny deck, muscular and without an ounce of surplus fat, but from his right knee to his shin was a scar not quite six inches long. She was immediately curious, remembering there were times when she had noticed a slight limp, but hadn't dared question it. The scar, she felt sure, must be in some way connected with his life here, with the fatalistic attitude he had admitted to, and the mysteries still surrounding him. Her fingers hovered over it a moment with an urge to touch the deep mark, instinct telling her that it had affected him more seriously than the physical sign showed, but she resisted and lifted her eyes.

A fly settled on his nose and he flicked it away with a whiplash movement of his hand, then relaxed again with apparent contentment, his eyes still closed. Minella watched him, absorbing every line of his face, and a melting feeling made her half afraid to draw breath. In a few short days he had become the hub of her existence, and somehow even Greg had assumed a minor role. The delay over his arrival hadn't been nearly as disappointing as it would have been a little while ago because it meant she and Sam could be alone longer. But why ever had she welcomed it?

Her heart was beating loudly in her ears, drumming out a rhythm which couldn't be ignored. Every time she looked at him it happened, and she had to face the fact that dislike and hate were only words she used to disguise emotions she refused to recognise. This man, who had carried her to safety, now held her entirely. She wanted to be with him, to be excited by his magnetism and the fight she had to put up to resist it. She had to be teased, caressed, wanted. Yes, that last implication was the crucial one. No use wrapping up the idea in any fancy words. She wanted Sam Stafford, even though she knew only heartbreak lay in that direction. She pushed the thought aside and stopped looking at him.

Gradually she became calmer and the crude revelation was relegated to the back of her mind, though it continued to throb like a pain. Considering all that Sam had done for her, a temporary lack of common sense was only to be expected, but he must never know. His laughter would echo as far as the cliffs and shake the delicate pink tamarisk flowers. But she couldn't stop herself expressing her gratitude. She leaned forward and let her mouth brush over his like thistledown.

'Thank you, Sam,' she murmured.

He opened his eyes lazily and gave a quizzical smile, giving himself time to fathom the reason for such an unexpected token. Then he raised himself on one elbow and returned the kiss with one equally soft against her cheek before putting an arm around her and drawing her down beside him on the deck. She sighed and rested her head against his shoulder, the close contact bringing a fervent warmth to her body, and her hand fell limply on his chest. On that perfect afternoon there was nothing more she wanted to make her happiness complete, except perhaps to tell him, and that would have ruined everything.

When five o'clock came they were back again at the airport, waiting for the flight from São Miguel, and this time there was no hold-up. Minella walked beside Sam feeling eyes upon them, conscious of his attraction which made women turn for a second glance, his confidence, his air of authority making anyone he spoke to show respect. She wanted to tuck her hand possessively through the crook of his arm, but laughed at herself when she remembered that that was exactly what Consuelo had done last night. Nothing had really changed. Sam was Sam, and when he obviously had the pick of women on Fayal it was no good hoping for more than a temporary paternal-type affection from him, if indeed she had any wish for more.

The plane touched down and soon passengers were crossing the tarmac in twos and threes. Minella scanned them eagerly for the first glimpse of Greg, filled now with excitement at their imminent reunion. Then she saw his fair head, his broad smile and ambling gait, and ran forward to meet him, forgetting Sam. And to her great joy she saw that he was not alone. Annette was with him.

As soon as she could reach him she was clasped in Greg's arms, babbling incoherently in her excitement, and then it was Annette's turn. She had never been so pleased to see anyone in her life, and they fussed over her as if she had been gone for months. Linking her arms through theirs, she led them through the lounge to where she had left Sam.

'I can't wait for you to meet the man who saved my life. Well, he didn't actually do the rescuing, but he looked after me when I was ill and contacted you as soon as he could. . . .' She went on talking, looking for Sam, who wasn't in the same place.

'We've got a lot to thank him for,' said Greg. 'Lucky for you there was an Englishman around. Trust our Minella to get into a scrape and come up smelling of lavender!' He cuffed her ear playfully.

'A bit of a mixed metaphor,' laughed Annette, 'but I guess it's true.' She gave Minella a sideways glance. 'This man, did he provide you with the new clothes?'

'He lent me the money because I'd nothing to wear. Greg, please can you square up with him later?'

'So I'm to be the loser,' Greg teased.

'You'll get your money back even if it takes all my next pay cheque.'

'And the pendant?' Annette queried. 'Did he buy that for you?'

Minella fingered the fine gold chain and her face coloured. 'It was a present,' she said, surprised that her sister-in-law had missed nothing. She sounded almost cross.

Sam was at the entrance, standing with his back to them so as not to intrude on the family reunion, but at the sound of their voices he turned with a lazy smile.

'Sam, this is my brother Greg,' Minella cried. 'Greg, meet Sam Stafford.'

The two men exchanged polite greetings and Minella turned to introduce her brother's wife, who was hovering in the background, head averted.

'And Sam, this is my sister-in-law, Annette. Isn't it marvellous she could come, too?'

Annette came out of the shadow, tall and poised and with an aloof, almost disapproving look. Oh, no, Minella thought, surely she wasn't going to play the heavy older sister bit. It wouldn't be like her at all.

'We're greatly indebted to you, Mr Stafford,' she said, offering her hand.

Sam took it slowly, and Minella's exuberance dimmed when she saw his reaction to Annette's beauty. He stared at her with open, incredulous admiration, his eyes gleaming, and held her hand much longer than necessary. The wretched man was blatantly flirting with her before a word was spoken!

'It *is* marvellous you could come, Mrs Farmer, and I'm glad you find Minella in such good spirits.' He turned to Greg. 'I did my best to keep her quiet and rested as the doctor suggested, but it's hard to keep track of her sometimes. Is she wilful when she's at home?'

'She's always had a mind of her own,' laughed Greg. 'And she certainly looks fine now. We're more than grateful.'

'You must let us pay the doctor's bill,' said Annette.

'There's no bill to pay,' said Sam. 'Henrique is a friend of mine, and he was part of the rescue team. He's become quite fond of our little waif. Can't think why.'

Sam draped a casual arm round her shoulder as they talked about her, the words light and amusing, but Minella found nothing funny in the repartee. He was talking of one girl and thinking of another. She shrugged his hand away, angry and embarrassed.

Sam just couldn't takes his eyes off Annette.

CHAPTER SEVEN

IT had been a difficult evening. An underlying tension was so strong that Minella couldn't believe she was the only one who felt it, yet on the surface it had been a happy enough occasion.

'I hope you'll stay on for a few days,' Sam said at dinner. 'There's plenty of room in my house, and there's something I'd like to take you to at Ponta Delgada. I know you'd enjoy it.'

Greg protested, 'We've put you out enough already.'

'Nonsense! I don't see many English people and it's a wonderful change. Makes me realise how much I miss my own country.'

'Why don't you go back to it?' Annette asked.

Her lovely face was half hidden behind the sultry curtain of golden hair that swung to her shoulders. By day she wore it coiled at the back of her head, but this evening she looked more alluring than Minella had ever seen her. Sam was aware of it too. He went out of his way to see that everything was to her liking when dinner was served, making quite sure she liked the dryness of the wine. It was almost as if they were alone, but if Annette felt uncomfortable about the extra attention she didn't show it. She handled the situation with cool dignity. That was the impression she gave, but as Minella watched closely she became convinced that Annette was playing some kind of game. She was certainly not impervious to Sam's interest, though only Greg seemed not to notice.

'I don't know that I'd want to give up the lifestyle I have here,' Sam admitted.

'You've certainly got a beautiful home,' said Greg, looking around.

'He's got a powerboat and a cottage by a lake as well,' Minella added.

Annette raised her eyebrows eloquently. 'Has he indeed?'

Lamplight glowed on the antique silver cutlery and porcelain dinner service, and a young girl with black plaited hair and white dress and apron waited on Sam Stafford's guests. He knew how to entertain graciously, as if he had always been used to luxury and took it for granted, but he frowned at the mention of his possessions.

'I wasn't referring to material things,' he said. 'No doubt I could keep up the same standard in England if I wanted to, but I could never be at peace with myself the way I am here. I've discovered how to relax and let the world pass me by, and how to accept the inevitability of everything. I doubt if I could cope with the rat race any more.'

'You mean you'd still live here even if you had no money?' said Annette.

His eyes met hers across the table. 'There's no question of it.'

'But you're an artist,' protested Greg. 'Wouldn't it be more exciting to hold exhibitions in England and meet all the right people in the art world?'

Minella sighed, irritated by her brother's inability to understand, and surprised at herself for understanding so well when only yesterday she had even questioned his honesty.

'The art world wouldn't want to know me,' said Sam. 'In literary terms I'm a hack, and it's only tourists who buy my stuff for souvenirs. As for excitement, I can do without it.'

'Has your philosophy changed, then?' asked Annette.

'In what way?'

'I have the feeling you might once have lived an exciting life.'

Sam leaned on the table, long fingers stroking the

close beard which softened his jawline. 'Mrs Farmer, or may I call you Anne. . . .'

'My name is Annette,' she corrected.

'Annette, then, perhaps we can discuss what my life is or was at some future date when it won't make boring dinner conversation. But let me just say I would only go back to England if something affected me deeply enough to make life here unbearable. The chances are remote, and a short while ago I wanted nothing more than to spend the rest of my days here, but things happen unexpectedly. It may be that I shall have to return if that's the only way to gain what I desire more than anything else.'

'You'll be welcome to stay with us for as long as you like,' said Greg. 'We can never repay you fully, but we can offer you hospitality any time you need it.'

'Thank you. I don't want any repayment, but what I *do* want may not please any of you, so let's not pursue the subject further.'

He had distributed uneasiness among them which remained long after the subject was dropped. He refilled their glasses and diverted them with tales of his experiments in winemaking, which had never been successful, but though they laughed it was not with the original lightness. And the way he continued to look at Annette made Minella so angry she wished she had the courage to douse him with the contents of her glass. Apart from the insult to Greg it was a disgraceful way to behave. And the devil looked as if he enjoyed every moment of the discomfort he caused!

Was it only that afternoon she had lain with her head on his shoulder, full of warm new emotions that expanded her heart and sent dreams of glorious fulfilment cascading through her mind? Minella watched Sam concentrating all his charms on her sister-in-law and was disgusted, not only with him, but with herself for having been so naïve. She had fallen into the trap just like all the other women, in spite of her initial good

sense. The wisest thing she had done was escape with
Vasco after the brutal kissing session he had forced on
her. The thought of it now brought a pain to her chest
and she couldn't eat another thing.

'I trust you'll try some *aguardente*,' Sam was saying.
'It's a local brandy with which our Minella is already
acquainted, but I don't think you'll find it too strong
after a good meal.'

She looked up quickly and his blue eyes sparkled
with amusement as they met hers. She froze. Surely he
wouldn't ridicule her in front of everyone? The
familiarity in his smile set her heart racing with fear
that he might be cruel enough to disclose her escapade
with Vasco, and Greg wouldn't approve of that at all.
But he turned without mentioning it, and proposed a
toast instead.

'To us!' he said, reverting to his preoccupation with
Annette. But before Greg could become suspicious he
widened the address. 'And to Minella, my little
Sparrow, who unwittingly brought us all together.'

'To Minella!' they laughed, and raised their glasses.

'May we never regret it,' she said, with more
seriousness than her tone implied, for she was filled
with foreboding. When Sam tipped his goblet against
Annette's and held her gaze for more than a decent
length of time the significance didn't escape her.

Minella went up to her room ahead of the others,
leaving them to joke with the lightness of good
companions before parting for the night. She couldn't
stand it any longer. It was so obvious that all Sam had
in mind was how pleasant it would be to change places
with Greg and share Annette's bed. And after the
aguardente even Annette showed signs of wishing for
the same thing. Minella felt sick.

Sam was a womaniser. She ought to have known that
from the first. Any woman would do for him, but a new
arrival on the scene, especially one as beautiful as
Annette, was exciting game and it didn't matter who

got hurt in the chase. She had believed him when he said Consuelo only worked in the studio, and that Benita was only his housekeeper. How many more Azorean women did he keep for his amusement? Thank goodness she had found out the truth before it was too late, because she had come dangerously near to blurting out words of affection when they were together on the boat and he would soon have turned them to his advantage. How safe would she have been tonight if Greg and Annette hadn't arrived after all?

A strong wind had sprung up since nightfall and the fig-tree outside her bedroom window cast eerie shadows on the moonlit wall. She stood in the middle of the floor and watched the leaves splay their stubby fingers and produce caricatures that matched her chaotic thoughts, fascinated, yet repelled by that fascination. The shadows were ugly and destroyed the beauty which created them.

It wasn't Annette's fault. With the uncanny sensitivity of one closely involved in a situation, Minella had understood exactly how Annette felt, being suddenly introduced to such a dynamic creature. If Sam Stafford chose to exert his powerful male personality it would take a strong woman to remain unaffected. Annette had tried. The frigid reception she had given his first overtures were commendable, but who could hold out against the flattery of so much personal attention? The fact that Annette had softened visibly towards the end of the evening was what worried Minella, and all her fury was directed at Sam because it was her beloved brother who was eventually going to get hurt, and he certainly didn't deserve it.

She put her hand to her throat and touched the gold chain Sam had given her. Grasping it tightly, she was tempted to drag it from her neck and stretch every link beyond repair, but though her knuckles turned white she resisted the temptation and presently undid the catch. For a second the memory of his touch weakened her, but she thrust it aside, determined never to react that way again.

With the pendant bunched into her palm she left her room and went across the corridor to where she had heard Sam slam a door after bidding his guests goodnight. Temper made her careless of propriety and she almost burst into his room without knocking. She stopped just in time and gave the thick wood panels an imperious staccato rap. He came immediately, as if he had been waiting, yet no way could he have mistaken the knock for that of a would-be lover. He had already removed his shirt and the belt of his pants was in his hand.

'I don't want any gifts from you, Sam,' Minella declared icily. 'You can take this back and save it for a more accommodating recipient!'

She pushed the pendant at him, and when surprise made him delay in taking it, it fell to the floor and lay glittering between them.

'You'd better come in,' he said, stooping to retrieve it.

'No. I've nothing else to say. Goodnight.'

Before she was aware of his intention his hand shot out and grasped her wrist, dragging her over the threshold before she could put up a fight.

'Now you can tell me what this nonsense is all about,' he said, as the door closed firmly behind her.

She was alone with Sam in his bedroom. Her legs were quaking, but she took a deep breath and faced him with all the confidence she could muster. Let him know right away how low he had sunk in her estimation!

'You behaved abominably this evening, and I'll thank you to leave my brother's wife alone,' she said, firing the first shot like David attacking Goliath. 'If only you could see what a fool you look ogling every woman within reach! You're always telling me not to be juvenile, but what on earth do you think *you* look like, acting as if you're a star-struck teenager? At your age! You. . . .'

'Hey wait a minute!' Sam stopped her in mid-flow, astounded by the outburst. 'Just what have I done to merit all this?'

'You don't need me to tell you. From the moment you saw Annette you made a dead set at her, but let me warn you, Sam Stafford, she's much too good for you, and she's got more sense than to fall for your ridiculous philandering!'

'I'm sure she's a very sensible girl,' he agreed.

'Then respect her, and my brother, and don't go chancing your luck!'

Her temper was at its height and she didn't trust herself to say any more, so she swung round, intending to make a haughty exit, but it didn't work that way. Sam wasn't a man to take abuse quietly and she hadn't allowed him to speak for himself. The belt in his hand flicked round like a whip, encircling her waist with stinging accuracy, and she was drawn back towards him, helpless.

'Don't think you can issue orders in my house, Miss High-and-Mighty, especially not to me,' he said, his voice dangerously low. 'If you've finished having your say it's time you listened to me. I don't need any reprimands for showing your sister-in-law the kind of courtesy she would expect from me. She's a very beautiful woman and should be treated as one. Your nasty insinuations spring only from your nasty little mind, and I'm sure she would be as amazed as I am that you object to my treatment of her. Had you behaved more like a lady yourself I might have shown you the same courtesy.'

Minella wriggled against the restricting leather. 'Thank goodness I've been spared it!'

He now held each end of the belt in his hands, imprisoning her within inches of his chest, and she could smell the expensive spray he had used when changing for dinner. His shoulders gleamed and the muscles of his arms rippled as he tightened his hold of the belt and forced her even closer until their bodies touched in spite of her resistance. His powerful thighs burned against hers through the thin material separating them, and she felt as if she was suffocating.

'Now you can tell me the true reason for this nocturnal visit,' he said, a sensuous undertone richly softening his voice. 'Was it because you were afraid I might take someone else to bed instead of you?'

She gasped, unprepared for the crude change of tactics, though she ought to have known it was inviting trouble when she knocked on his door. She faced him defiantly.

'That's the coarse sort of comment I'd expect from you,' she snapped, hoping he couldn't tell that jungle drums were beating in her ears, setting every pulse throbbing. 'I don't suppose you think of much else. You're despicable, and I wish I'd never met you!'

'Do you?' His eyes narrowed but the corners of his mouth twitched. 'Do you really wish that, Sparrow? Tell me honestly, if I asked you to come to bed with me you'd come, wouldn't you.'

'No, no, no! How dare you say such a thing! And if you try to force me I'll scream. My brother will hear, and it won't do your reputation any good.'

'Or yours, little one.'

Sam was laughing as she struggled, and a moment later he let go of one end of the belt. She staggered from him, not quite losing her balance, and thankfully reached the door.

'You really are a beast!' she said, with gritted teeth.

'And you are a hypocrite, as I shall one day prove. Now get back to your room before I offend you even more by calling you childish, and don't interfere again in my affairs.'

'I'd rather ruin my reputation than let you ruin my brother's marriage, but you wouldn't appreciate the sacrifice.' She lifted her chin. 'All I ask, in the name of decency, is that you leave Annette alone.'

She returned to her room, feeling as if she had just escaped being buried by an avalanche. But at least she had had the last word and he was left in no doubt about her sentiments. She poured cold water into the big basin on the washstand, stripped off her clothes and sponged her body until it was cool, wishing the amenities of Sam's house extended to a shower. It was not until she was rubbing herself vigorously with a fluffy pink towel that she began to smile. A line from a book of Paul Gallico's came into her mind, vividly describing the reason for feline behaviour, and one cat had advised the other, 'When in doubt, wash.' Wasn't that exactly what she had done?

Lying in bed, too stressed for sleep, she stared once more at the wall shadows and tried to straighten out her confusion over Sam. Everything she had said to him was right, every epithet deserved, and she wasn't really in any doubt at all, so why did her treacherous body behave contrary to every moral code she believed in? Even now she could remember every coursing thrill his first kiss had caused, though it ought to have sickened her, and icy water had had little effect on her raised blood heat, for which he was directly responsible. With shame she re-lived the excitement such close contact with him had aroused and imagined how it would be now if she had allowed licentiousness to override wisdom. She closed her eyes and pressed the lids with her finger tips until flaring colours dispelled images she didn't want to see. Yet at the back of her mind there still remained gentler pictures.

All that really mattered was that there should be no further developments where Annette was concerned, because if there were Minella was at a loss as to what she could do. But part of the answer came in the most unexpected way.

She had dreaded seeing Sam in the morning, but as it

turned out it was not Sam who was the problem. Trouble started early in the morning when Minella went out into the courtyard early and was met by Greg, who was obviously not in a good mood.

'I saw you come out here and I thought now would be the best time to have a few serious words with you in private,' he said, sounding like a Victorian father figure.

'Of course, Greg,' she answered, and wondered what reprimand he intended giving. Last night he had chastised her about removing her lifeline during the storm at sea, a mistake which had almost proved fatal, and there was no doubt if he hadn't been so relieved to see her he would have made a much greater issue of it. So what now?

He had a worried frown. 'I want to know exactly what's going on between you and this man Stafford. Before you make a single denial, Minella, let me tell you I'd been to the bathroom last night and I saw you going into his room.'

Drops of moisture from the leaves of flowering creepers dripped spasmodically, plopping with insistence in the humid air, and there was a pungent smell of damp vegetation. Minella couldn't believe she had heard Greg's accusations right, yet if that was what he had seen it was a natural conclusion to have drawn. But he could have had more faith in her.

'Nothing is going on, as you put it,' she said indignantly. 'Sam has done a lot for me, but he's older than you are and he's treated me as a sort of ward.'

Forgive me if it's not quite the truth, she murmured to herself.

'That's not what it looked like to me,' said Greg. 'I wasn't born yesterday, Minella, so don't try and play the innocent. I know these are enlightened times, but you're not the type for permissiveness.'

'How do you know what type I am?'

He was about to make another angry retort, but saw the rebellion he was up against and knew it would have to wait. 'I've always hoped you wouldn't have the same frivolous attitude to life as Mother,' he sighed. 'It's never seemed that way till now. All I want is for you to have a happy marriage like mine and Annette's.'

It was then that she knew the answer. Much as she disliked the idea, she would have to play up to Sam as if there was a grain of truth in what Greg had said, then he wouldn't suspect it was Annette who was the attraction. Oh, what a lot of complications the wretched man was causing! It was a great pity Greg had already accepted the invitation to stay until the end of the week.

Sam was late for breakfast. He had been down to the harbour for fresh fish. His hair was blown, his face glowing from the brisk walk, and when she saw him Minella had to concentrate hard to keep anger alive. He really was very good-looking in that rugged, masculine way. He stood in the doorway holding an enormous fish aloft, and it was as if he was an actor on a stage captivating an audience.

'I wish I could say I'd caught it myself,' he declared, 'but the bigger one got away. The pick of the catch always eludes me.'

Everyone laughed, setting the tone for the day, and to Minella's relief he was on his best behaviour. She went and sat beside him at the table, smiling sweetly.

'That's because you try too hard and make yourself obvious,' she said, her cheeks dimpling. 'Be thankful there are plenty of lesser fish.'

He gave one of his mighty roars of laughter. 'I was going to suggest we take out the boat on a fishing expedition. I'm told there's a big shoal of mackerel off the bay. It'll serve you right, Sparrow, if I decide not to take you with us!'

The next two days passed without incident, an infectious holiday spirit catching up with them as soon as Maria, the housekeeper, produced the first packed hamper. Minella was happier, assured that Sam had given her warning serious thought because he didn't attempt to step out of line, but she never relaxed her guard. If they were all out together she made a point of walking with him, sitting next to him for meals, staying around so there was no risk of him being alone with Annette. He knew, of course. She could tell by the wicked glint in his eye when she purposely put herself between them. There were times when she caught him looking at Annette, thinking himself unobserved, and there was more than casual interest behind the scrutiny, which worried Minella considerably, but there was nothing else she could do about it except remain vigilant and hope Annette was unaware. It was an air of restrained familiarity developing between them that troubled her more, as if in spite of her care they had managed to talk alone and get to know each other, but it gradually became an easy friendship in which Greg was included and she fell in with them thankfully so that it became a companionable foursome.

Plans were made for them to take the powerboat over to Ponta Delgada, which was the capital of São Miguel, the largest island of the archipelago.

'I know a good hotel where we can stay for a couple of nights. I've already made the arrangements,' said Sam. 'And on Sunday I'll take you to a bullfight.'

It was Minella who protested. 'Oh, no, I wouldn't like that at all. It's too cruel!'

He slipped an affectionate arm round her waist and smiled at her alarm. 'Don't worry, Sparrow, Portuguese bullfights aren't like the Spanish ones. None of the bulls are killed, and you'll find it great fun, I promise.'

'You've been before, then?' asked Annette.

'Many times. I enjoy it immensely. There's so much atmosphere.'

Minella was still not sure, but she couldn't spoil it for everyone else, so she made up her mind not to think about it until the time came, and there were so many other interesting things to see it was not difficult.

The people of Ponta Delgada called it a city, and

Minella loved it straight away. There was a cosmopolitan air about it which could be felt as soon as they put into harbour. Launches were coming in from deep sea fishing excursions and tourists waited to be photographed with catches of enormous swordfish and tunny, but the yachts with bright-coloured sails made her feel almost too much at home.

They had had to make an early start from Horta to cover the considerable distance between islands, so by lunchtime the exhilarating trip and sea air had made them ravenously ready for lunch at the luxurious hotel where Sam had booked them in. Minella wondered who was footing the bill. Each mouthwatering dish was superb, but by the time the dessert was served she had ceased to care about expense. It was the most wonderful pineapple she had ever tasted, the inside scooped out and mixed with peaches and passionfruit brandy, then topped with chocolate and nuts.

'I never knew pineapple could taste that good,' she said, reluctantly setting down her spoon when the last fragment was gone.

'That's because it's grown locally,' said Sam.

'What, here, in Ponta Delgada?' asked Annette.

'It's one of the island's industries.' Sam looked at his watch. 'Tell you what, if you're interested I'll phone my friend Alban da Costa and if he doesn't mind showing us round his greenhouses we'll take a taxi out there this afternoon.'

All agreed it was a splendid idea. Sam's friend proved to be overjoyed at the prospect of English visitors, and Minella was relieved at having something interesting to do to take her mind off the bullfight tomorrow.

Alban was tall and dignified, more like a country squire than a grower of pineapples. He bowed over the hand of each lady and proudly greeted them in English, but his knowledge of the language was not sufficient for him to be clear about Minella's relationship to Sam. As Greg and Annette were not within hearing distance when he made the mistake of assuming she was his intended wife, the mistake went uncorrected.

'She is so pree-ty,' he said, his index finger beneath Minella's chin. 'You are lucky, my friend.'

'Oh, but. . . .' she began.

'Yes, I'm very lucky,' Sam agreed, and took hold of her hand.

Alban led the way to the first building with a sloping whitewashed roof. He began to tell them about the three phases of cultivation, Sam translating, but she couldn't concentrate on difficult things like the types of fern, heather and peat from the mountain heaths needed to make suitable soil when Sam's fingers were still twined through hers. She didn't know what Greg would think, but the touch of her palm against Sam's was too stirring for sensible conduct. Just this once she would permit herself the luxury of enjoying the physical response he inevitably awakened.

It was fascinating to see the fruit actually growing. The buildings were connected by paved pathways between pineapple beds, and Alban explained each stage of cultivation, from the planting out of shoots at the base of the parent plants, to the time of ripening which was so important. He introduced them to his *estufeiro*, the supervisor, who showed them how the plants were subjected to a smoking process after about four months, to ensure that all the fruit ripened at the same time.

'Then after one year the pineapples are ready for you to eat,' said Alban.

'Mmmm,' said Minella, licking her lips, 'with peaches and passionfruit brandy. When I'm home I shall remember how divine it tasted.'

Sam translated, and Alban raised his wiry grey eyebrows. 'Ah, but you will have pineapples of your own when Sam starts to grow them like this on Fayal.'

They were on their way back to the hotel when Greg questioned Alban's statement.

'Are you really going in for pineapple production, Sam?'

'I've given it thought,' said Sam, 'but it's costly out here. It's such an intensive process, as you've seen, and it's hard to compete with open-air growers in hotter climates.'

'Oh, but it's exciting,' cried Minella. 'I'd love to live on one of those grand estates and watch pineapples grow.'

'Then you'll have to stay out here and we'll start a family business in the old tradition,' he laughed, looking from Greg to Minella, and finally Annette, in a contemplative way.

'With Minella it would be a five-minute wonder,' said Greg. 'She wouldn't be happy for long without her boats.'

'There are yachts in Horta,' Sam reminded him.

'It wouldn't work,' said Annette, decisively.

'We'd make it work, wouldn't we, Sparrow?'

Sam helped her out of the taxi outside the hotel, a quizzical smile tipping up the corners of his mouth, but Minella didn't answer. She was lost in a momentous discovery. The thought of leaving the Azores and never seeing Sam again was too great a pain to dwell upon, and she looked at him in stricken perplexity. Knowledge of such vast importance made her oblivious of darting cars and hurrying people, forgetful of her brother and his wife, uncaring of everything except Sam.

'Minella, do you feel all right?' asked Annette, seeing her sudden pallor.

She blinked hard, trying to dispel the vision of herself and Sam working together on a shared project, in harmony with each other. Sharing their lives.

'I'm just a bit tired,' she murmured. 'Too much sun.' Thank goodness Sam had gone to pay the taxi driver.

'You've been doing too much since the accident. Better take it easy this evening.'

She wanted to be alone to reconstruct all that had

happened since the morning Sam had carried her up the beach, selfishly counting each moment like a miser with gold. Hadn't she known even then that her heart had found a home? A compelling force had flowed between them, raising her low body temperature more thoroughly than the blankets Sam had wrapped her in, and she had ceased to be afraid. She remembered, too, how she had called for Greg when the fever was at its height, and Sam had held her close and kissed her hair, soothing her more lovingly than any brother. And in temper he had kissed her later, warning her not to expect brotherly treatment from him. Was it really only concern he felt for the waif he had rescued, or could there possibly be deeper motives?

She watched him peel some notes off a bundle and give them to the taxi driver, declining change.

'I'm okay,' she said to Annette. 'You go on. I'll wait for Sam.'

For the first time she resented Annette. She was jealous of Benita and Consuelo for being involved in his life. Then she re-lived the experience of her hand in his the way it had been today, and the simple, compatible pleasure it had given her couldn't be denied. He was an irascible man, arrogant, and too attractive to women for his own good, but none of his faults could lessen the way she felt about him.

The taxi pulled away. Minella stood on the pavement, the brilliance of the white, sun-drenched wall opposite blinding her to all but Sam as he walked towards her, unaware. Nor did the city people who pushed between them realise the cruelty of keeping her from him.

She put her hands on her hips and said to herself: 'What a helluva place to discover you're in love!'

CHAPTER EIGHT

ANNETTE was waiting for her when she went up to her room to change for dinner.

'I want to talk to you, Minella,' she said, in her schoolteacher voice which was reserved for difficult moments, and there was a sharpness about her that extended from the firm set of her mouth to her neatly placed feet. Minella had never seen her like this before.

'You'd better come in.' She totted up the events of the day and couldn't think of any reason why Annette should look so angry.

The shutters were still across the window to keep out the heat, but now the sun had gone from her room she folded them back, hoping for some air.

'Minella, you don't seem to be aware of it, but you really are making a fool of yourself over Sam Stafford,' Annette said severely. 'I know you're very young, but that's no excuse.'

Completely unprepared for the accusation, Minella stared at her blankly. Coming on top of the revelation a few minutes before, the words seemed to bear no relation to the matter and she wanted to put up a barrier between herself and any intervention until she had had time to sort things out.

'I don't know what you mean,' she said, 'and I object to always being told I'm very young. Several girls I know of my age are married and have children, so you've no right to bring age into any quarrel you intend to pick. Has Greg asked you to speak to me?'

'No, but he would want me too if he knew how concerned I am. I've watched you playing up to Sam, always behaving as if you have priority, and anyone can see he finds it very amusing. I can't help wondering what went on before your brother and I arrived.'

So this was what happened when you tried to protect someone! She'd known it was a risk, but hadn't realised it would have such far-reaching effects. Because of it she had alienated Annette and fallen in love with Sam. What a mess!

'It's none of your business,' she said crossly, and turned away, hoping that would be the end of it. Let Annette think what she liked!

But the terse remark infuriated the other girl and she caught hold of Minella's shoulder, swinging her round.

'I'm making it my business,' she snapped. 'You're my husband's sister, but I've always felt we were close enough to be real sisters and that gives me the right to try and talk some sense into you. If you think he'll ever marry you, Minella, you're very much mistaken. The Sam Staffords of this world don't go in for matrimony.'

'Who said anything about marriage? You're jumping to conclusions. And how can you possibly know what Sam wants to do? You've known him even less time than I have.' Minella was glad the hotel bedroom was so impersonal. Surely nothing of this would stay in her memory for long. She slipped her feet out of the mules and hoped the cool, tiled floor would effectively ease the burning temper she had to control.

Annette was undeterred. 'That ridiculous display of hand-holding this afternoon didn't go unnoticed. You tried to make Sam's friend get the impression you belonged to him, that's for sure. Well, I've met men like Sam. They're all the same, out for what they can get. He's probably been using you as payment in case we don't have the money to foot the bill you're costing him.'

'Annette!' Minella was horrified. If she had had a bucket of water thrown over her she couldn't have been more amazed. Whatever was wrong with her sister-in-law? For what purpose was she digging up these degrading suggestions. 'That's a disgusting thing to say, and I demand an apology!'

Annette paused uncomfortably, aware that she had gone too far, and sat down on the edge of the bed. 'All right, perhaps that was a bit dramatic, but I had to jolt you out of that sickly cow-eyed look you give him. It makes me want to throw up!'

There had been differences of opinion between them, but never harsh words like this before, and the anger they provoked was cruel. Minella was close to tears. It was so uncalled-for. The bulk of Annette's grievance was based on supposition, and there had to be more behind her objections to make her so vindictive. There had to be a stronger reason for this extraordinary slanging match. She studied her a moment and gradually recognised the flickering emotion in her eyes as a need for self-protection rather than concern for someone else. Annette was curiously sensitive about Sam.

'Why?' Minella asked, quietly. 'Why do you want to throw up? Is it because you're jealous?'

The tables were turned. Annette was on her feet again, eyes blazing, but the retort she had been on the point of making was sucked back on a gasping breath. A hint of fear touched her as she saw adult argument taking shape between her and the girl she had looked upon as a kid sister.

'I don't give a damn for him,' she said. 'It just makes me furious to see you believing in him with such innocence. He'll only hurt you.'

'Then I needn't have bothered to try and divert him after he made such obvious passes at you the evening you came. He was bowled over—and don't try telling me you didn't know it. I saw you react to him, and you're married. Oh, he's a *very* attractive man, but so is my brother, and he's the one I won't allow to get hurt.'

Annette suddenly wilted. The blotches of angry colour that had stained her fair skin gradually faded.

'You're right,' she agreed, 'neither of us must hurt Greg.' She held out her arms in a gesture of apology impossible to ignore and they hugged each other fleetingly, but it was not an easy truce. 'Promise me you won't lose your heart to Sam Stafford. I'm sure he's not worth it. He's too worldly and too old for you, and Greg wouldn't approve.'

'Don't worry, I can take care of myself,' said Minella, with careful diplomacy.

When Annette had gone she felt as if she had weathered another storm, and she stood by the window trying to clear her mind of the conflict. There was something odd about Annette's outburst. It was as if she had been bottling it up for some time and couldn't contain it any longer, but the reasons she had given could almost have been an excuse for something deeper. She wished she understood what it was. Admittedly she was eight years younger than Greg's wife, but the difference in their ages was not sufficient to make their outlook on life at such variance. While she had every right to disapprove of her sister-in-law playing around with another man and jeopardising her marriage, there was very little reason why Annette should disapprove of a harmless relationship between two single people, unless she had a personal interest in the affair. Could she possibly have become instantly infatuated with Sam Stafford?

'The sooner we're away from these islands the happier I shall be,' she had said as she went out of the door, almost as if she was afraid of something.

There was a discordant sound in the street below, like tin cans being pulled over the cobbles. Minella hadn't expected to see a bullock cart in the city, but one came trundling by, stacked high with sugar-beet. The pace was slow and careful, and no doubt the load would reach its destination safely.

Slowly, carefully. That was the way she had to tread now with Sam. Interesting that Annette's appraisal of him matched her own so well. Surely they couldn't both be mistaken? But as she thought about it quietly in the aftermath of that verbal storm she knew that had he been any other kind of man she wouldn't have fallen in love with him.

Both girls were unusually quiet at dinner, and it was assumed they were tired after a long day.

'It's a pity we can't spend longer here,' said Sam. 'I could have taken you to the valley of Furnas. It's quite famous for its exotic plants and you'd think you were in a jungle. And there's the Seven Cities. . . .'

'Seven besides this one!' Greg exclaimed.

Sam laughed. 'No. But there are seven lakes, where perhaps there were settlements in the early days. The two largest are very deep and though they flow into each other one is bright blue and the other green. It's quite extraordinary. There are plenty of legends about them, but the one I like best is about a shepherd with green eyes who fell in love with a princess who had eyes of royal blue, and when they were parted for ever the tears they shed flowed into the two lakes and gave them their colour.'

'That's lovely,' sighed Minella. 'I wish we could see them.'

Sam was at his most persuasive, and even Greg wavered. 'The business is in good hands. Another couple of days wouldn't matter.'

'We can't,' said Annette firmly. 'Mrs Douglas agreed to cover for two weeks only, and Minella must certainly get back to her job.'

'What exactly *do* you do?' Sam asked. 'Other than mess around in boats, of course.'

Minella looked down her nose with mock indignation. 'I sell them. And I'm very good at it.'

'She's right,' said Greg, with a smile. 'She started in the office of Stave Brothers at eighteen and they discovered she had a natural aptitude for convincing people that a boat was something they couldn't possibly do without. She's now part of their top sales team.' He said it proudly and leaned over to give her hand an affectionate squeeze.

'You mean she's one of those glamorous birds who decorate the stands at boat shows,' said Sam, raising his eyebrows.

'That as well,' Minella agreed.

But there was no smile from Annette. 'You wouldn't recognise her at work. She's cool, efficient, and extremely smart—which is more than I can say for her at the moment.'

Since only Minella was aware of the double meaning there was no lull in the conversation, and the sumptuous meal lingered on like all good continental meals. They were entertained by guitar music and folk dancing which involved a lot of stamping of the feet, and a beautiful girl who looked like a gypsy sang the *Pezinho*, which Sam said was one of São Miguel's oldest songs. Minella watched him while the girl was singing, absurdly afraid this might be another one to take his fancy, but it seemed to be only the music he was enjoying.

Afterwards she walked along the Avenida Goncalo Velho with Annette, while Sam took Greg to check the powerboat. The wide sea-front embraced the curve of the harbour, and in the fading evening light she had to concentrate on the black and white stone patterns on the pavement to stop herself seeking out the place where she knew the *Samanne* was moored. Being without Sam even for a short time was now lamentable and showed her all too clearly the heartbreak permanent parting was going to cause.

'But there'll only be a large brown pool where *my* tears are shed,' she chided herself. 'And it's no good thinking there'll ever be a blue one beside it, because he'll hardly miss me.'

The day of the bullfight dawned like every other day in the Azores, the humid ocean air promising a full quota of sunshine, but Minella awoke with a premonition that trouble was on the way, and she wasn't far wrong. To start with, Greg didn't come down to breakfast. He had always been subject to migraine attacks, and having suffered all night with one he still felt too ill to do anything except stay in a darkened room.

'When he's like that he only wants to be left alone,' said Annette.

'Which means I shall have the pleasure of taking out two beautiful women today,' said Sam, after words of sympathy. Then he gave her a very personal smile. 'Tell him I'll look after you well.'

Minella had been toying with the idea of making the excuse of a headache herself to get out of going, but not if it meant giving Sam and Annette a day to themselves. She must have been looking uncertain, because Sam turned to her as an afterthought.

'And I'll look after you, too, Sparrow, never fear. Can't trust these handsome matadors! If you fall for any I want to make sure it's the right one.'

'I'm not likely to do that,' she assured him.

His hand was on the back of her head, ruffling her hair, and the touch sent shock waves cascading down her spine.

They arrived early at the bullring. Sam had people to see and he wanted to be sure they had good seats. It was a sizeable place where there was room for two or three thousand spectators, and in spite of herself Minella found the atmosphere of the crowd infectious, though it hadn't escaped her notice that the bullring was directly opposite the cemetery. When Sam disappeared she looked round and absorbed the colourful scene, finding it exciting after all.

Girls were arriving by the score, laughing and coquetting, and many of them carried spectacular bouquets. Shortly before the entertainment was due to begin Sam came back with flowers for Minella and Annette.

'These are for you to throw to the bravest bullfighter,' he told them.

Minella buried her nose in the fragrant blooms and wished they had been a gift for herself. It was a sheer waste to shower them on men who were foolish enough to fight bulls. She stared above them at the circle of sand, dazzling in the heat, and prayed he had been telling the truth when he said there was no killing.

And then she was aware that he was introducing her to someone.

'This is Carlo,' he said, standing aside for a young man to move into a vacant seat beside them. 'He's one of Alban's sons and he usually goes into the ring, but today he's hurt his back.'

'So my good friend Sam is going to fight the bull for me,' said Carlo, grinning broadly.

'What!' exclaimed the girls in unison, and Minella's heart plummetted quicker than a lead weight.

'You're joking, aren't you?' said Annette.

'No. Sam fights bulls well. He has done it many times.'

'Is that true?' breathed Minella.

'It is,' said Sam. 'It's a sport I've become very interested in since I came here to live.'

The tiers were full and music played. Last-minute scuffles broke out as boys who had found a way in without paying were thrown out again on their ears. Then a trumpet sounded and the crowd went wild with delight as the first bull careered into the ring. Minella closed her eyes. It was several minutes before she opened them again and saw that it was a group of men in the ring who were only trying to catch the bull.

'You see,' said Sam, 'I promised it would be fun.'

There was so much shouting all around her she hardly heard him, but he reached for her hand. She slipped it into his so naturally and gave no thought to Annette on the other side of them.

She watched a man dash at the charging bull,

grasping its neck as he flung himself forward between the horns. It was the second time he had tried it. The first time the bull veered away at the wrong moment and the man was thrown to the ground and dragged along. This time he succeeded in keeping his hold until the rest of the men brought the beast to the ground, and the crowd roared. Minella's knuckles were white as she gripped Sam's hand.

'I don't want *you* to do that,' she said fearfully.

'I won't get hurt, little one.'

He was a braggart on top of everything else. She was sure it was pure exhibitionism and he would find her state of nerves amusing, but there was nothing she could do about it. His eyes were on her. The intense scrutiny fevered her blood and sent her heartbeats out of control, but she was not going to add to his amusement by letting him see the effect he had on her. Every nerve bristled with anger and frustration and she hardly knew how to stay in her seat. Her lovely mouth hardened into an unsmiling line and she continued to stare straight ahead until the battle of wills became so strong one of them had to be the loser. The pull of Sam's magnetism was too strong for her. Slowly Minella turned her head. The blue eyes concentrating on her with such force showed not a trace of amusement, and the impact stunned her momentarily. As her gaze met and fused with his all aggression fled away and she was filled with an astounding peacefulness quite beyond all previous experience.

Nothing had changed. Waves of cheering filtered back into her ears where all sound except her heartbeats had been blocked out. The last of the crazy men, with their anxiety to match their prowess to animals they had penned up for hours, played the trick of leading a cow into the arena to distract the bull. A minute later the ring was empty.

Minella was trembling inside like a tree shaken by a summer gale, but she felt like singing. Surely he wouldn't

look at her like that, with fire glowing in his eyes, if he
didn't feel more than patronising affection. The spell
was broken and he turned his attention to Annette,
giving her the chance to indulge in a secret study of that
masterful head and commit each detail to memory,
from the curls clinging damply to the nape of his neck
to the trim beard that contoured his chin. A few grey
threads glinted silver in the smudge of dark hair above
his upper lip, and she tried to imagine him clean-
shaven, but the picture didn't fit. Part of his sex-appeal
stemmed from the classic growth of hair sculptured
cleverly beneath that fine nose and straight, strong
mouth. In the heat of the afternoon she melted with
longing for the feel of that mouth on her own.

The next part of the proceedings was soon under way
and the laughter of the crowd became a charged,
breathless excitement with cheers for the first matador
who strutted into the ring with a flourish. Girls held
flowers ready to throw even before he had faced the
bull, so he was obviously popular. Minella tensed with
apprehension that flared up in anguish as Sam
murmured to the girls that he must leave them.

For a few minutes she watched the antics of the man
in the arena, the curving sweep of his heavy cloak that
made the girls gasp as he baited the bull. Then she
covered her eyes as it charged and narrowly missed
striking him with its horn. Nothing on earth could
make her stay and watch Sam face that kind of danger.
Annette was captivated, as mesmerised by the spectacle
as the Azorean girls, and was deaf to Minella's plea to
leave, so she tugged at Carlo's sleeve.

'Please don't let Sam go in there,' she begged. 'I can't
bear it!'

Carlo hated being distracted. 'He do it for me
because I owe money and if I not pay, my father find
out. He is a very good man.'

Everyone around her stood up, waving and gesticulating as the excitement mounted, and the solid wall

of people between herself and the only way of escape gave her a terrible feeling of claustrophobia. She had to get away. Close to panic, she pushed Carlo aside and fought her way to the steps. The resistant mass of people stood firm against her, hardly giving an inch and oblivious of her desperate cries to let her through. She thought she was going to be crushed. Then like a miracle she heard her name called.

'Minella!'

The sweet sound was like music amidst the cacophony of Portuguese, and she searched frantically in the direction from which the call came to find the person who knew her. A few seconds later a hand grasped her arm and she turned, half sobbing, to see the familiar and oh, so welcome face of Vasco Hernandez, the last person she had expected to see at a bullfight in Ponta Delgada. She fell against him, her legs shaking so much she could hardly stand.

'Vasco, I never thought I'd be so pleased to see anyone! Please, get me out of here!'

He grinned at her, not trying to answer against the impossible din, and somehow he managed to lift her, shouting something in Portuguese as he did so. Like magic the crowd parted and made way for him to carry her away from the throng. He put her down as soon as they were through, and it was such a relief she threw her arms round his neck and hugged him.

'That was unbelievable!' she cried. 'How did you do it?'

Mischief danced in his dark eyes. 'I told them that you were pregnant and feeling ill.'

'Oh, Vasco!'

They were at the back of the stadium and she sank down on a bench, collapsing with relief and convulsive laughter at his audacity.

He laughed with her. 'I am so happy to see you. I thought you had gone back to England and I would never see you again. My heart it was breaking. I could not believe it when I saw you.'

'Nor I.' She gulped back the last frenzied giggle. 'What are you doing so far from home?'

'Once a month I come to the bullfight with my friends,' said Vasco, still staring at her as if he was dreaming. 'They wonder how I come to know such a beautiful girl. If I were a matador I would dedicate a bull to you.'

Minella shuddered. 'That's the last thing I'd want you to do! I don't like bullfighting at all. I didn't even want to come.'

'Is that why you are so unhappy?'

'Partly.' She couldn't tell him that Sam was taking Carlo's place on the programme and she was so afraid for his safety she couldn't bear to watch. Vasco would think her mad, and he might even be right. Loving Sam was a form of madness. Trying to appear normal, she told him instead about Greg and Annette coming to Fayal to collect her and being invited to stay on.

Vasco scowled, his handsome olive-skinned features darkening with displeasure. 'I wish you were not with that man. He makes me feel ... how do I say ...?'

'Inadequate?' Minella suggested.

'I do not know what that means. To him I am small, you understand.'

'Yes,' she sighed. 'He makes me feel like that, too, sometimes. And yet he can be so wonderful.'

'How can you say that!'

'Do you know what he's doing now?' she asked. 'He's going into the ring to fight a bull instead of a boy called Carlo who has hurt his back and needs the money to pay off debts which his father mustn't known about. Isn't that just heroic ... and ridiculous?'

There was another trumpet fanfare and then Sam was announced. There was a hush of surprise from the crowd, followed by an enthusiastic burst of applause. Obviously he was no stranger to them, and he had their respect. Minella's face drained of colour.

'Why did you not tell me?' Vasco was saying

impatiently. 'He is great with the bulls. I must not miss this.' Then he saw the colour of her cheeks, and incredulous emotions chased across his face. 'You are in love with him!' he accused.

When she didn't answer he shrugged and got to his feet, hovering indecisively. He was afraid to leave her, but he had come to enjoy every minute of the spectacle. He pulled her up beside him.

'Come! You must see him for yourself.' There were cheers and shrieks of delight from the tiers and he dragged her to the rear of the stand where there was still a good view. 'This is a *garraiada*. No one gets more than bruises. See!' He pointed at the fearsome-looking animal which seemed to be charging round the ring in all directions. 'There are no barbs in its neck. It is not a cruel sport, but it needs skill and strength, and Sam Stafford has both those. Perhaps that is another reason why I do not like him.'

In spite of herself Minella became fascinated, caught up in the surging encouragement Sam inspired, even finding it funny when once he had to run for the barricade, almost seized by the heels. But after split-second summing up he gained mastery, getting the measure of the furious bull. After a few minutes of play, first in kneeling position, and then with a dazzling display of sweeping cloakwork which was sheer poetry to watch, he seemed to be able to do anything he liked with the animal. It brought the crowd to its feet, roaring and cheering, and there were so many flowers thrown in the ring they carpeted the sand. Minella waved her arms, so proud of him she had to shout like everyone else, and when the bull-catchers finally came in to get the bull down she was laughing with delight.

'Oh, you were right, Vasco, he's absolutely marvellous!' She hugged him again, this time with exuberance. 'We must go and find him straight away.'

Vasco protested that there were still two more items to see, but Minella didn't care. All that mattered was getting to Sam. She wanted to be with him, to share this moment of triumph and let all these people know that Sam was hers. Above all, whether it was right or wrong, she wanted to tell him that she loved him. Her heart was bursting with love which he just had to return. There couldn't be any doubt about it after the way he had looked at her. It had felt as if he was drawing her very soul to him and merging it with his own, and she needed him more than she had ever needed anyone in her life.

She still had flowers in her hand, and though she was too far away for them to reach him she flung them towards the ring, seeing them scatter over the heads of girls who could only admire him from afar. But as she did so a worried hush gradually spread over the spectators and she saw that Sam was still in the ring, a group of men surrounding him. A small man carrying what looked like a medical bag joined them, and everyone was silent.

'Vasco, what's wrong?' Minella gasped, fear returning.

He stood on tiptoe and craned to see above the heads now straining forward to see what had happened.

'It looks as if his knee is bleeding,' he said. 'They are helping him up now the doctor has tied something round it. He is all right, I think.'

'You think!' she cried. 'I must go and find out.'

She darted from his side. If Sam needed help he must have been hurt quite badly because he would be too proud to accept assistance unless it was absolutely necessary. She hadn't seen anything go wrong. He had outwitted the bull at every turn, except perhaps once just before the catchers came in when it had come dangerously close to goring his leg. It hadn't appeared to touch him, but maybe the horn had grazed him after all.

She didn't know which way to go and some youths drinking from wine bottles jostled her, purposely barring her path. The harassment continued until Vasco caught up with them and once more he came to her rescue. But time had been lost, and when they eventually reached the gate used by the bullfighters it was to find a throng of fans gathered and there was no hope of getting near.

Minella was not tall enough to see what was going on and nobody understood her when she asked if they would let her through. Not that they would have done. Everybody wanted to see Sam Stafford, and all of them were unlucky. A spokesman told a girl at the front, who passed the information back, that Sam had been taken to hospital. When Vasco told her, Minella's eyes widened in alarm and her mouth was so dry she could hardly swallow. How awful!

'You'll have to take me there,' she said. Then she remembered Annette. 'But first I've got to find my sister-in-law and tell her. She'll be so worried. She's got long fair hair and we were sitting near the front. I ought not to have left her.'

'I will find her,' Vasco volunteered. 'It should not be difficult. You go to the entrance and we will meet there.'

When he had gone Minella made her way to the main gate, away from the crowd which was now returning to the tiers for the final events of the afternoon. She found a place in the shade to wait, and her stomach churned with apprehension. She had certainly been right with her premonition when she woke this morning. It was turning out to be a disastrous day.

She couldn't understand what had gone wrong with Sam. It hadn't appeared as if the bull could possibly have done serious damage, but for some reason he was bleeding badly. And then she remembered the scar on his knee, the long, jagged mark which had intrigued her that day on the boat. An old wound. Sometimes old wounds needed only slight pressure on them to break open, with nasty results.

Vasco was a long time. Minella tapped her feet impatiently, wondering whether he was engrossed in the proceedings which were under way again, forgetting what he had gone back for. She was considering trying to find a telephone to ring for Greg when at last he came back, alone.

'She is not there,' he said, spreading his hands palm upwards in a gesture of resignation. 'I spoke with Carlo, who said she also has concern for Sam.'

'Oh, what a muddle!' Minella exclaimed. 'Then we'd better get to the hospital. Have you enough money for a taxi?'

He took some crumpled notes from his pocket. 'It is all I have.'

'Good,' she said, taking them from him. 'I'll repay you this evening. Now can you get one for us?'

'I am to come with you?'

'Would you let me go alone?'

He was contrite. 'Of course not. I will look after you—I always do.'

Now that something definite had happened she was no longer nervous. It occurred to her that she ought to have spoken to someone in charge in case Sam had left a message, but he had been rushed away so quickly he probably hadn't even thought of it.

Luckily there were taxis in the vicinity waiting for the afternoon sport to finish, but even so it took longer to get to the hospital than she would have liked. She sat on the edge of the seat as the car bumped along, cross with everything that got in their way, and too preoccupied to talk.

It was busy at the hospital, people ambling in all directions with the visiting time look about them. Vasco asked about Sam at the reception desk. The woman chatted to him, obviously telling him which way to go, and he started to translate for Minella when something else she said made his eyebrows lift in surprise.

'She says he is in a private room on the first floor

waiting for the doctor to put stitches in his knee, and then he can go. She also says his wife is with him!'

For a moment Minella looked mystified and was about to protest that there had been a mistake when she realised what must have happened.

'I expect Annette came with him after all,' she said, with a relieved smile. 'They would think she's his wife because she's English.'

The stairs echoed with their footsteps and they were afraid to speak because every sound seemed to carry and become magnified, so they merely looked at each other and stifled laughter as they crept along the first floor corridor looking at room numbers.

And then they heard voices from an open doorway. English voices belonging distinctly to Sam and Annette.

They were far enough away to be unobserved, partially hidden by a screen in the corridor. Minella saw Sam on his feet looking none the worse for the accident, and Annette with her back towards them, but something about the way they faced each other made Minella pause, instinct cautioning her to wait, and she restrained Vasco with a warning touch.

'All right, Anne,' she heard Sam say, 'we'll continue to play it your way, but I still think Greg should be told.'

'No,' said Annette. 'I don't ever want him to know. I begged you not to let anyone suspect, but you might as well have shouted it from the rooftops.'

'How could I help it? That first evening I really thought I was dreaming!'

Annette reached up and put her arms round his neck. 'Please, Sam, don't be cross. I'm much too happy to risk spoiling anything.'

'If that's the way you want it,' said Sam, and bent his head to kiss her.

Minella was rooted to the spot, staring at the oblong patch of light where the two were framed as if acting out a motion picture. But this was no film, no make-believe. Their treachery filled the air and she was afraid to draw breath in case she was contaminated. Her anger was equally potent. She would never have believed Annette could play such a devious game. Sam, yes— Sam could never be trusted. But Annette had sworn she wanted nothing to do with him, denounced him for what he was, and Minella had actually believed her.

She thought the hospital smells of ether and disinfectant would stay with her for ever. Her skin seemed to be soaking it into every pore as time stopped still. Harsh hospital noises vibrated her eardrums, piercing into the fragments of conversation going through her brain like static-induced repetition on a record, yet she couldn't utter a sound.

Slowly she became aware that Vasco, too, was motionless, mesmerised by the scene as if it affected him personally. And when Annette moved her head so that her face was visible, he murmured an exclamation on exhaled breath.

'He-ey! That girl!' His eyes were bright with revelation. 'She is the one in the portrait!'

CHAPTER NINE

'TAKE me back to the hotel,' muttered Minella, in a hoarse whisper. 'Please, Vasco, before they see us. I can't stay here a minute longer!'

'You do not wish to speak with them?'

She shook her head, and his disappointment showed in the woeful expression she would have found funny at any other time. He had made the most exciting discovery and was not to have the opportunity of following it through. One look at the pain in Minella's eyes was sufficient to convince him that the shock she had suffered was genuine but still he hesitated.

'Just for a moment more I want to look at her,' he said.

But Minella had gone. The late afternoon sun on the pavement outside dazzled her after the gloom of the hospital and she leaned against a wall, fighting for breath as if she had been running. But there was no escape. The troubled thread she had thought would be broken as soon as they left the Azores had become a web of intrigue with Sam at the centre, and she was caught up in it, lured by the same attraction that had entangled Annette all those years ago. She didn't know which was worse, the impression Sam and Annette had given of embarking on a holiday affair, or the truth which Vasco had innocently uncovered. Her head was spinning, and she couldn't begin to think clearly until she reached the solitude of her room.

Vasco came round the corner a few minutes later and found her, and he was laughing as if they were children playing hide-and-seek.

'Why you not wait for me?' he asked. 'I could not come away until I had seen her properly. I think perhaps she is not quite so beautiful as in the painting.'

Minella clutched at the slight ring of doubt. 'Are you sure it's the same girl, Vasco?'

'Yes, I am sure,' he said. 'She is older, but I do not make a mistake.'

'Could it have been painted about eight years ago?'

He debated the question, then nodded slowly. 'I think yes.' They started to walk and he put his arm round her waist. She didn't object; it was good to have his support. 'It is a beautiful painting, and once I thought I would never meet a girl like that. But now I think you are much nicer.'

His flattery was irresistible, and in spite of the load on her mind she was able to smile.

'What I do not understand,' Vasco went on, with a perplexed frown, 'is how this girl comes here as your brother's wife. You did not know she is the one Sam keeps hidden away in his hut?'

'How could I even guess?' said Minella. 'Everything seems to have suddenly turned upside down. All I know is that Annette was once going to marry a man, but he was injured and lost his job, then disappeared, and she never saw him again. Sam must be that man. It all fits. His boat is even called *Samanne*, don't you see?'

They turned into a street she recognised and the hotel was a little way up the hill.

'What are you going to do now?' he asked.

She sighed. 'I don't know. The only time Annette ever talked about Sam ... about her love affair, I was so upset that someone could walk out on her like that I vowed I'd really give him a piece of my mind if I ever came across him. Well, now I have, and I'm in love with him, too ... or I thought I was. I'm so confused. And there's still so much mystery about him.'

'You are too good for him,' Vasco said vehemently. '*I* am the one who is in love. Stay with me.'

He really was very sweet when he tried to play the

Latin lover, and she wished she returned his feelings, but suddenly she felt twice his age. She looked at him with almost maternal affection as they stopped outside the hotel entrance, and the germ of an idea came to her.

'You know I can't stay,' she said. 'But I would like you to take me out on your motorbike before I fly back to England. Will you come round to Sam's house for me?'

His dark eyes flashed with new hope. 'I will be there at dawn,' he cried, his chest expanding. 'We will fly like a winged machine across Fayal and find a place to be alone!'

Minella laughed and squeezed his hand. It was so much more comfortable being with a boy she liked and with whom she could joke lightheartedly.

'We don't leave here until well after dawn tomorrow, and I'd rather you didn't career across the countryside like a mad thing. I want to be able to get back to England all in one piece. Now,' she became serious, 'have you enough money to last until you get back to Horta?'

'I have my plane ticket, and my friends will lend me any money I need.' He looked at his watch. 'I must hurry or I will miss the special plane that takes us home. And I will count the hours until I see you again.'

She ought to have looked in on Greg before going to her room, but after standing outside his door a moment she knew she was in no mood to talk about the bullfight, or what had followed afterwards, and she went on up the stairs to seek the privacy she so desperately needed.

Until she had seen Annette she couldn't decide whether to admit to the discovery she had made. Annette had begged for secrecy. The reason for it became more complex as soon as she gave it thought and she flopped down on the bed face downwards, wishing that this whole adventure had never started.

She wished more than anything that she had never

met Sam Stafford. Her life had been happy and uncomplicated before he came into it, but now nothing was predictable except heartbreak. She had never been really conscious of the age gap until now, but important things had been happening to him while she was still only a child, and he must be finding her youthful inexperience very amusing.

She still couldn't associate Annette with his past. It seemed impossible that they had known and loved each other years ago, yet the facts fitted too well for it not to be true. Given a little time for it to sink in she would be able to accept it. What was completely unacceptable was the obvious sign that they were still in love. Annette had said Greg mustn't be told, mustn't be hurt, but Sam wanted to shout it aloud. How gullible she must be! After the shameful way he had treated her she ought to have shown him no mercy, let him know that when he walked out on her it had been for good. Weakness was no way to deal with a man like that.

Minella got up and groaned, afraid to examine her feelings any more closely. Her head ached and she bathed her eyes with warm water, hoping to erase memories of her own yearning for Sam. It was too easy to condemn Annette. Sam was the one who was as black as she had painted him, but that fatal charm was hard to resist and if he chose to use it to gain what he wanted who could be blamed for succumbing. All Minella knew was that *she* was certainly not going to be fool enough to fall for it again.

There was time for a bath before dinner and she ran one calmly, determined not to give way to the pain attacking her temples. A few minutes' relaxation in a hot bath would ease the tension away and put her in a better state of mind to face people later. She stepped out of her clothes and into the water, mentally blocking all thoughts of Sam, and the steam rising all around her created a soothing mist into which she seemed to float, discarding all immediate problems.

The minutes ticked by and she was dangerously sleepy, sinking further into the rosy haze made by a setting sun and pink bath salts. And she didn't hear the knock on her bedroom door. The knock was repeated, and unheeded. Minella's eyes and ears were closed to the outside world and she was oblivious to everything, so it was a shocked awakening when the plug was suddenly pulled out and water gurgled round her toes as it began to run away. She sat up with a start and blinked her eyes before letting out a horrified yell, because Sam was standing there in the mist, drops of moisture already sparkling on his hair and beard. His large frame, magnified by the steaminess and made slightly out of focus, seemed to completely fill the bathroom. He held out a pink towel to her.

'What do you think you're doing!' he demanded. 'I've rescued you once from drowning. Do I have to keep on doing it?'

'How dare you come in here!' she shouted. 'How *dare* you! Get out this minute!'

The water was draining away rapidly, leaving her unprotected, and he didn't even have the manners to look away. Her body, already glowing from the warmth of the water, now burned as if she was in a furnace.

'Your door was unlocked and there was steam coming through the keyhole,' he said. 'How was I to know there wasn't a fire? You'll be the death of me, if not yourself!'

His eyes travelled from the tip of her nose, down over her neck, lingering on her small but well-formed breasts, and she hurriedly drew up her knees and hugged them against her like a pixie, wishing she could slide down the plughole with the rest of the water.

'Have you no sense of decency, Sam Stafford?' she cried, making a grab at the towel.

'None,' said Sam.

But he turned and opened the window while she stood up and wrapped herself in the fluffy pink bath towel. The steam cleared quickly and she went to step out of the bath, but the porcelain was slippery and in her hurry to put a respectable distance between them she skidded over. With a gasp she landed in a pool left by the departing bath water, and when Sam saw what had happened he hooted with laughter. Before she had the chance to regain her balance he leaned into the bath and scooped her up in his arms, carrying her back to the bedroom squealing like a scalded cat.

'Stop that noise,' he warned. 'I'm not hurting you.'

She continued to struggle, kicking violently and hoping the towel would stay firm. He stopped by the bed, and when she cried out even louder he silenced her by the simple method of covering her mouth with his. She tossed her head, trying to escape him, but the pressure increased until she gradually went limp in his arms. His lips against hers sought to arouse her and the fight was lost. Forgetting the towel, Minella raised her arms and slid them round his neck, her fingers furrowing through his wiry dark hair, and she abandoned herself to the glorious, pulsating turmoil that rushed through her body as he crushed her to him. If there was never another moment like this in her life she would be sure this one was never forgotten. But as his mouth trailed kisses along the curve of her throat and down to her breast she began to struggle again in panic, realising just where her own reaction was leading, and she stretched her head until she could bite the lobe of his ear viciously.

He dropped her on the bed. His eyes smouldered with dark, insatiable emotion.

'If you weren't so innocent, Minella, you'd know that that's no way to stop a man doing anything. Quite the reverse.'

She was rigid with the effort to control her anger and confusion.

'Isn't it enough that you've got Annette?' she blazed. 'Do you collect women like scalps? You're not safe to be near!'

'What makes you think I've got Annette?' A cold, suspicious ring crept into his voice.

'I came to the hospital. You were kissing her.' Tears she was ashamed of him seeing welled up and refused to be quenched, lying like diamonds on her lower lids before spilling over on to her cheeks. 'Why can't you leave us both alone?'

He was motionless, and the verbal retaliation she had expected didn't come. Instead his eyes held hers and a deep sadness replaced the previous fires. He looked tired.

'I'm sorry, Sparrow. There are things you don't understand, and I can't explain.'

He bent forward and gently stroked the tears from each cheek with the pad of his thumb, and the longing to take his hand and hold it to her lips was so strong she jerked her head aside.

'I understand all too well,' she snapped. 'You've no feelings except the basest ones, and you don't care if you hurt people. Now, will you please go away!'

He lifted his head and it was as if a mask fell into position, wiping everything demonstrative from his expression and leaving it hard and inscrutable.

'I came to apologise for this afternoon's fiasco,' he said. 'Things happened in such a rush and no one knew where you'd gone. Annette was very worried about you. I hope she knows you're safely back here.'

'I haven't seen her,' said Minella. She was about to tell him that Vasco had taken care of her, but it would have aggravated the situation, so she kept quiet about it. 'I'm sure you'll be glad of an excuse to go and tell her how you've found me ... if Greg isn't with her, of course.'

It was a cruel remark, and for a tense instant she thought he would slap her, but he did nothing. A moment later he turned on his heel and strode away, unable to disguise a limp brought on by his damaged knee. When he had gone Minella propped herself up on her elbows and stared at the door, her heart pumping painfully, and she wished she'd commented about his injury, but in her present mood she was inclined to think it served him right.

Greg was fit again the next morning, full of disappointment that he had missed the fun and excitement and eager to make amends. By the time the *Samanne* was under way, heading back for Horta, he was at the controls, handling the powerboat as if he'd been doing it for years, while Sam reluctantly sat back.

'He isn't even supposed to put weight on that leg,' said Annette anxiously, 'and he's been walking around ever since we left the hospital. The doctor was afraid it might bleed again and it could be difficult to stop.'

Nothing much had been said about the emergency treatment Sam had had to receive. He refused to talk about it other than to make light of the incident and both Minella and Annette had avoided precipitating a discussion. Clearly Annette was worried, but awkward questions would have been difficult to answer, as Minella now realised.

Minella had spent a restless night. She had wanted to speak to Annette and tell her she knew the truth, but it would have been an intrusion. She watched them at dinner, two people who had once been in love and planning to marry, but now bewildered by their feelings after the long estrangement. Did Sam regret it? He was being particularly careful to treat her with casual friendliness, but Annette was in danger of letting the extent of their familiarity be known. Her concern for him after the accident was obvious, though she tried to hide it.

The one thing Minella longed to know was how Sam had acquired such a bad knee wound in the first place. It must have been a traumatic experience if it had cost him his job and necessitated exiling himself on a lonely Atlantic island. It had to be quite a story, but she didn't think she was ever likely to hear it. The truth was probably unpalatable anyway. If it had been impossible to stay in England and marry the girl he loved it must have been a shameful business. He was an insensitive brute!

But Annette was still in love with him, in spite of her marriage. She had said she was too happy to risk spoiling everything, so Greg must never find out. Poor Greg, blissfully unaware that his wife was playing a dangerous game! Minella's heart ached for him, which made it easier for her to harden herself even more against Sam Stafford.

They were back at the house in Horta in time for lunch, but Minella had little appetite, and was glad everyone was too engrossed with their own problems to notice that she was abnormally quiet. No matter how much she tried to think of other things her mind returned to Sam and Annette with increasing curiosity. Somehow she had to help Annette get this fever out of her system, but it would be difficult unless she knew whether Sam's love had ever been genuine. If it had, and he was serious about her now, what chance was there of saving her brother's marriage?

One way to find an answer, she was sure, was to see for herself the portrait Sam had painted all that time ago. Vasco had idiotically fallen in love with it, so it must be quite revealing. The idea of trying to see it had come to her yesterday, outside the hospital, and all she had to do was persuade Vasco to take her to the cottage. It shouldn't be too difficult.

She decided not to wait for him in the house. If Sam saw him he would try to prevent her going out. Keeping on her shorts and T-shirt, she said she was going for a walk round the harbour, pleading a headache that needed air. Greg and Annette were stretched out on loungers in the courtyard under the shade of the fig-tree, and Sam was nowhere about, so it was easy enough to get away. Minella was fairly sure which way Vasco would come and walked down to a corner to wait just before the time they had arranged, listening for the sound of his motorbike to announce his impending arrival, and he was there in a matter of minutes.

He greeted her effusively. 'Minelia Sparrow, I have been counting the hours and looking at the weather. I prayed nothing would stop you coming back to me.'

She wished he wouldn't call her Sparrow. It reminded her of Sam, and she wanted to forget him.

'There hasn't been any bad weather since the night I arrived,' she laughed. 'If I hadn't experienced that terrible storm I'd have thought you only had idyllic days.'

'The storm was Fate,' said Vasco, as she climbed up behind him. 'Where would you like to go?'

'I want to go to Sam's cottage.'

He looked round at her in surprise and his face lit up. 'That is a *very* good idea. Why did I not think of it myself.'

She hadn't expected him to agree with quite such alacrity. Persuading him to get a key for the hut by the lake would have to wait until later.

It was fun to be on the motorbike again, and the exhilarating feel of the wind tearing at her hair refreshed her more than anything else could have done. She clung to Vasco as he sped along the quiet roads and wondered how he would have liked driving in England. Judging by his love of speed and the risky way he took the corners, he would probably have been in his element doing top speed along a motorway, but though she wished he would go slower nothing would make her admit it.

At Minella's insistence they stopped to see Dr Porva on the way through Santa Silva. Vasco tried to dissuade her, saying it was the doctor's busy day, but Minella had grown fond of Henrique during their brief but eventful acquaintance and she knew he would be disappointed if she returned home without a word.

'You are right,' Henrique Porva said, 'I would not have forgiven you. When you came here you were a little drowned bird, but now you are dry and rested and ready to fly away. My thoughts will go with you.'

'I'll never forget you,' she told him.

'Nor I you. You must promise to come back one day.'

There were actually tears in his eyes as he hugged her tightly, but Vasco was impatient to be going again and he revved the motorbike sharply, hoping to draw her away from the door.

'She will come to see me,' he said.

Henrique looked from the girl to the boy and back again. 'I think not,' he said sagely. 'Minella has grown up in these days here. She has experienced much. But you are still very young, Vasco Hernandez.'

They had gone about a mile before Vasco made any comment. The doctor had insulted him, and he sulked in silence until indignation got the better of him.

'*You* do not think me too young, do you?' he called over his shoulder.

'Of course not,' Minella said, to pacify him. She felt his rigid back relax a little, the arms flex, the head lift. He had needed reassurance, and she smiled at the ease with which she could do it. If only Sam had need of her. Now it was *her* back that tensed. Sam was an arrogant, insular being who made his own laws and manipulated people to fit them. Forget him. Forget him! *Forget him!*

The cottage looked a tranquil haven, as beautiful as a calendar picture, and as empty. There was no sign of anyone around, and when Vasco tried the door it was locked.

'Benita will be with my grandfather,' he said. 'She does not live here when Sam is in Horta.' He studied the windows, pulling himself up on a ledge to look inside, then jumping down again. He grinned. 'It is as I hoped. We are here alone, and I know I can find a way in.'

Minella's heart gave an enormous lurch as she realised the new predicament she had unwittingly brought upon herself. No wonder Vasco had shown such surprised pleasure when she suggested coming to the cottage, such eagerness to waste no time getting here. She had led him to think she was keen to find somewhere where they would be comfortable and undisturbed, and what better place than this?

'Oh, no,' she gasped, 'I don't want you to do that.'

How could she have been such a fool? She had enough troubles to sort out without inviting more.

'It is all right, Minella Sparrow. There is a low window at the back that we can climb through. We will harm nothing.'

He took her hand, intending to lead her through the thicket of vines that covered one side of the cottage, but she dragged her hand away and stood firm. Memories of being alone with him on the powerboat came crowding back and she tried to reassure herself that he hadn't harmed her then, and he had had the same opportunity. But that day she had followed him innocently because she had nowhere else to go and he had been hesitant. This time he had the confidence of what he took to be her encouragement.

'Vasco, I don't want to go into the cottage. I thought Benita would be here. I . . . wanted to see her as well as Dr Porva. Don't you understand?'

He scowled, standing in front of her while perplexity narrowed his eyes and pursed his mouth. He obviously didn't understand at all and didn't like the idea of being thwarted, but then he tried a smile.

'You must not be afraid of me, Minella,' he said, in his most seductive voice. 'I will do nothing that you do not want.'

'Then please don't break in,' she said hurriedly.

A flock of birds invaded the quiet garden, flying up from the trees by the lake and squabbling raucously. Flashes of green distinguished them as canaries, but the song they sang was anything but sweet. The jangling noise jarred her nerves and increased her uneasiness.

Vasco continued to smile, but there was a contemplative look behind it. 'Then we will make love in the garden. Perhaps it will be even better. And this time Sam will not come to disturb us.'

He was not rough or frightening, but his arms encircled her and she knew it was safer to stay perfectly still than to try and get away. If she showed her nervousness too much he would get angry, and there was nowhere for her to run. Vasco would catch her as easily as a hawk after its prey. He tried to kiss her, but she put her hands firmly against his chest, warding him off, and she could feel his heart beating faster than her own.

'Vasco, do you know where the key is to the hut? We could go down there.'

'The hut? Is it better than here? More romantic?'

She paused, then decided to tell some of the truth. 'I must see the portrait of Annette. I must know why you fell in love with it.'

A big grin spread across his face, and his boyish good humour returned.

'Minella, you are funny! I am telling you that I love you, and you are jealous of a painting. It mean nothing now I have you.' He grasped her by the waist and swung her in the air. 'I am telling you you are more beautiful.'

'I'm glad,' she said, playing along. She even kissed his cheek. 'But I don't want you to love me like that, Vasco. I've got to go back to England tomorrow and we shan't see each other again. I don't want you to be hurt.'

He put his hand to his heart in mock despair. 'I shall be heartbroken. But I live for each day. We are here now and it is wonderful. If you want to go in the hut I will find the key.' He ran over to the patio and returned almost at once with a key on a loop of string dangling from his index finger. 'See, it is no secret. It hangs beside the door on a hook.'

He chattered all the way past the bougainvillaea-covered fence and down the steep path, but Minella wasn't listening. Sam was all around her. She could almost hear his voice berating her for being such an idiot, saying that she had always been a nosey brat and it served her right. When she reached the grove of trees that caught the shifting light and shimmered with magical colour she felt they ought to still reflect the pink and gold of dawn as they had that morning when he had caught her peering in the hut window, but now the sun was behind them, and they were richly green. A faint breeze rustled the leaves, like whispered criticism. She was trespassing, not only on his land but among his private possessions which he had kept hidden from prying eyes over the years, and she had no right here.

Vasco, still in a garrulous mood, was undoing the lock, and as the old wooden door opened on squeaking hinges she wanted to shout at him to close it again. Her breathing was shallow and she quivered with a new fear quite apart from the worry of being alone with Vasco. She was stealing into Sam's life, encroaching on personal revelations that were not for her eyes, and she was frightened of seeing the portrait of Annette. Frightened in case it revealed a depth of emotion for her which she no longer wanted to know about.

Sunlight poured into the little stone hut and Vasco held open the door, waiting for her to go inside, but she hung back.

'I don't think we should,' she said. 'Sam would be furious.'

'It does not matter what Sam would think. Who will know we have been here? You are a coward.' Vasco tossed the last disparaging remark over his shoulder as he went through the doorway.

He was right. She was magnifying things out of all proportion, and having come all this way with only one purpose it was quite ridiculous to let principles stand in the way. She followed him into the hut.

It was whitewashed inside as well as out and bone dry. Sam's painting materials were scattered over a bench at one end, just as he had left them last time he had been down here working, messy tubes of oil colour strewn around amidst papers and pieces of rag, but his brushes were collected together in a stone jar beside a half-finished canvas. She touched the brushes, her fingertips hovering over the bristles near enough to cause a tingling feeling to spread up her arm. These were things that Sam used lovingly. The tingling increased and reached her scalp.

Vasco was sorting among the canvases near the window, knowing what he was looking for, and when he couldn't find it he swore in Portuguese. Minella glanced up. On a shelf above her head was a framed canvas wrapped in polythene. She reached up and tipped the edge of the frame until it fell into her hands, nearly making her overbalance. Vasco looked round and gave a yell of delight.

'That is the one!'

Her hands were shaking as she removed the polythene. A moment later she was staring at the portrait of her brother's wife, knowing there had been no mistaken identity. It was a very glamorous picture. The blonde hair had light behind it, softening it, and the eyes were heavily made up, though the expression was not hidden. Annette's mouth pouted slightly, as if she was waiting to be kissed, and it was very definitely a study of a girl in love.

'Ah!' breathed Vasco, gazing at it reverently.

Minella closed her eyes, hating to look at the proof of Sam and Annette's love for each other. It was by far the best painting he had ever done, and she could see why it appealed to Vasco so strongly. Annette's delicate beauty had been cleverly captured and a sexual attraction added which must have been very potent when she was a single girl out to win Sam Stafford. No wonder Sam still wanted her! It must have been a great shock to him when she arrived out of the blue, still as beautiful, and married to another man. Not that he would let a little thing like a wedding ring stand in the way. If the portrait was of such sentimental value he couldn't bear anyone to see it, his memories of Annette must be even more so, and whatever the reason for his original desertion it counted for nothing now. Minella gave a choked cry.

Vasco held the picture in both hands, pleasure illuminating his face, but at the sound of her despondency he put it down carefully.

'It's all right, Minella Sparrow,' he said, misjudging her reaction. 'It is nice to see this again, but it mean nothing to me now I have you.'

He took her in his arms so abruptly she wasn't prepared. His young mouth stifled any scream she would have made and he pressed her against him so hard she couldn't move. Resisting with all her strength, she found the only way she could make an impression was to kick his shins, and this she did with such force he had to relinquish his hold.

'Vasco, stop it! I don't want you like this,' she cried. 'You're my friend, that's all.'

He was stunned. His black eyes didn't leave her face and he was hurt more by the rebuff than the attack on his shins.

'Friend!' he shouted. 'You asked me to bring you here, away from everyone. You make me think you want to be alone for the same reason as me. And now you are . . . ice! I do not understand.'

He tried to regain his hold, but she backed away quickly, only to find herself cornered. Fear gripped her because there was no way she could escape. He waited like a boxer, feet astride and arms ready to catch her whichever way she darted.

'Please, Vasco, take me home to Sam,' she pleaded.

She couldn't have said anything worse to inflame the situation. Sam's name was an anathema to him, and the muscles in his neck became cords of anger.

'Sam! Always it is Sam!' He grabbed the bench and tipped it up with a furious jerk, spilling paints and brushes everywhere. At the same time he drove a fist at Minella's stomach, not hard enough to hurt, but she was temporarily winded as she fell among the tubes of paint. 'Well, Sam can have you! And he can come and fetch you!'

He careered out of the hut in full temper, the noise of his going taking over from the commotion his action had caused. He slammed the door shut so hard it shuddered, and crumbling wood fibres showered to the floor. Minella couldn't get to her feet and she screamed at him to wait, but Vasco was deaf to everything but his anger.

To her horror she heard the key turn in the lock, and she reached the window just in time to see his fleeting figure disappear among the candleberry trees.

CHAPTER TEN

SHE returned to the debris and sat down. It had been useless to shout and her throat was hoarse, her fists sore from hammering on the door, but fear and anger had driven her to protest as loudly as she could, knowing it was futile.

Vasco would come back, of course. She pictured him reaching the top of the path and sitting on the motorbike saddle with the key burning his palm, and he would be sorry for what he had done. At any moment he would open the door, full of contrition, begging her to forgive him, which she had no intention of doing. He was impetuous and hot-tempered and it was cruel of him to frighten her like this, but he wouldn't leave her imprisoned for long. He couldn't possibly be that wicked!

The minutes passed and lengthened perceptibly. Insects buzzed in the cobwebbed rafters. The smell of oil paint, linseed oil and turpentine stung her nose and the heat was oppressive. She began to count her heartbeats, tried to empty her mind and stay calm, but solitary confinement was having a claustrophobic effect even in a short time. Her fingers clenched, the small bones cracking with a sharp echo in the quietness, and she listened with increasing anxiety for the sound of returning footsteps. They didn't come.

For a while she watched a shadow on the wall, concentrating on its movement in relation to a mark on the stonework, and the gap widened as the sun moved round. It was shining now through a narrow skylight directly above the shelf where Annette's portrait had been. Minella supposed she ought to put it back.

Why had she mentioned Sam? What on earth had

made her say such a stupid thing when he was the last person she wanted to see? Greg was waiting at the house and he was the one she always turned to. She and Greg would have to stick together from now on, because it looked as if it was just going to be the two of them. She drew up her knees and cradled them with her arms, resting her cheek against them as memories swamped her in despair. For days now Sam had filled her mind completely and it was impossible to forget him. She would never do that as long as she lived, but perhaps when the pain eased she would be able to think of him more comfortably and reconcile herself to this extraordinary trick of fate. It wasn't Sam's fault, or Annette's either, that they had been brought together again. All Minella longed for was to get away from this hut, and this island, where everything reminded her of her own folly. She wanted to be done with Sam for good. Except that she would be glad to see *anyone* right now to let her out of this infernal prison.

Damn Vasco! Where was he? It must be half an hour since he had stormed away, quite long enough for him to come to his senses. She got up again, fury mounting at her helplessness in this ghastly charade. It was hot in the hut. She felt as if she was suffocating and the walls were closing in on her. It had been exceptionally hot all day.

The door was old but solid. No amount of hammering on it had any effect and all she did was fill the already heavy air with more dust. The window offered no hope either. It consisted of a dozen small panes nowhere near big enough for her to climb through, and the frame was as solid and unyielding as the door. It was a waste of energy trying to make any impression on either, and she gave up for the second time.

She picked up the picture of Annette and studied it painfully. She had to get it back on the shelf out of sight, but as she reached up her foot slipped and the picture crashed to the floor. The gilt frame broke like matchwood. There was no glass to shatter, but the canvas lay face downwards with the backing loose, and if Sam found his masterpiece like that he would think it had been flung down in spite. There was nothing for it but to try to repair the damage. She lifted the picture, intending to replace the backing first, but when she examined it there was newspaper in the way, wedged in the hollow made by the canvas stretched over wooden framework. She pulled it out. What careless workmanship! She was about to throw the paper aside when a photograph on the folded front page caught her eye, and she drew in her breath. She was looking at a full page article about Sam.

The newspaper was eight years old and the headlines concerned an event that had happened one hot August day in London when an attempt was made on the life of a visiting head of State from one of the Far Eastern countries. He had been received with pomp and ceremony, and was leaving a lunchtime banquet when the would-be assassin stepped out of the crowd and fired. The first shot went wide of the mark and winged the ornate lintel a few inches to the left of the silk-robed figure it was intended to kill. The second, following instantaneously, hit Superintendant Sam Stafford of the Special Branch in the leg as he threw himself on the diminutive statesman, felling them both to the ground with split-second timing.

'This brave man saved my husband's life,' the statesman's wife was quoted as saying afterwards. 'No award is great enough to show our gratitude and admiration. He acted selflessly and with outstanding courage.'

The photograph of Sam showed him without a beard, the square jaw, firm mouth and shrewd eyes leaving no doubt about his ruthless authority. Strength was in every line of his face. Underneath was a potted biography. His father was a judge, his mother an artist,

and throughout history the family had bred tough sons.
It was no surprise when Sam trained for the Special
Branch and received mentions for dangerous assign-
ments right from the beginning of his spectacular
career. He had been purposely chosen as bodyguard to
the Head of State after rumours of extremist threats
had reached government ears, and it had been proved
there was no one more capable of doing the job.
Finally, it reported his condition in hospital as being
serious, but goodwill messages were pouring in and his
fiancée, Annette Moran, was by his bedside.

Minella lowered the paper, mesmerised by what she
had read and still seeing the picture of Sam in her mind.
To think she had once wondered if he might be a
crooked art dealer! Anyone in their right mind would
have known the kind of man he was, and if she hadn't
been blinded by her own conflicting emotions she
would have seen it, too. Only once had he hinted at
anything like the truth, and she had thought he was
joking. Oh, Sam! What a wonderful, heroic thing to
have done! She re-read the page again, and found her
eyes stinging with unshed tears.

She felt very small and insignificant. She had had the
temerity to fall in love with someone so far beyond her
reach it was laughable. When she thought of the
dangers he had faced, the people he had mixed with, the
respect and fear he had commanded, she was amazed he
had even looked at her at all. No wonder he lost
patience with her easily! She dreaded what his reaction
would be to this latest escapade.

And then she decided she didn't care. Annette had
been with him after he was wounded, probably out of
her mind with worry, and all the thanks she had got
was a disappearing act as soon as he was fit to leave.
Perhaps he thought she wasn't good enough for him
after all the praise and adulation he received. The tale
about him losing his job must have been pure
fabrication. He was a swollen-headed, arrogant devil,

out to cover himself in glory. Why else would he have treated them to that vain display yesterday at the bullfight?

Yesterday. It seemed like a month ago.

Minella glanced at the newspaper once more, then put it carefully back with Annette's portrait. It might be wiser not to let him know she had seen it, for while it answered many questions that had puzzled her, it posed even more, and she was determined not to become further involved. She pressed her fingers to her temples. Her head was throbbing.

She went back to the window and peered through the trees for a sign of movement that might mean someone had come to look for her, but the trees were motionless. To occupy her mind she tried to remember what Sam had told her about them. Candleberry trees, he had called them. They were candleberry myrtle, but the first settlers had thought they were beech and named them *faya*. They grew very quickly and protected the orange groves from thieves better than stone walls, and because they covered the landscape, the island was called Fayal after them. These were protecting Sam's property. She imagined them getting taller even as she watched shadows play among the leaves, and they seemed to be closing in on her. She had never felt so small and alone in her life.

It was no good kidding herself. Vasco had locked her in this small stone prison and abandoned her. He wasn't coming back, and she might never get out.

She felt sick. Apart from being so hot she found she was thirsty and craved for a drink. Her throat was parched, and she was beginning to get very frightened. Vasco's fiery Latin temperament had a lot to answer for. What frightened her more than anything was the fact that no one except Vasco had any idea where she was, and when they missed her they wouldn't know where to start looking. She could be locked up here for days. If she didn't have a drink soon she didn't know how she was going to survive, but there was no sign of a tap anywhere.

'I'll have to pace up and down,' she told herself. 'Keep moving, Minella, and try not to think about anything.'

Like a prisoner in a cell she marched from one end to the other, her chin held high, and she was subconsciously murmuring a prayer when she became aware of a strange, terrifying sound. It was all around, like an express train speeding towards her and shattering the silence which in itself had become something of a nightmare. She covered her ears with her hands and screamed, thinking she was going mad. A few seconds later she was literally thrown off her feet, as if the floor had become a rug and some unseen force had lifted it up and given it a good shake. She tried to clutch at the wall, but it moved away from her, bulging outwards and finally disintegrating with the pressure of the shifting roof. The whole place was about to collapse. Before she realised it was an earth tremor she wasted precious seconds staring in horror, too petrified to scream again. Then she clambered frantically over falling masonry, desperate to escape.

Dust choked her. The noise of sliding tiles and breaking timber deafened her, and she grazed her legs on the bricks as she scrambled over them, but she was clear of danger. She wasted no time looking back at the damage, but started to run as if demons were after her, making for the path up to the garden, and she was almost at the grove of candleberries when she heard her name called in urgent warning.

'Minella, get away from the trees! There'll be another one!'

She stopped in mid-flight, not knowing which way to run, and she was shouting for Vasco at the top of her voice. Suddenly the earth was sliding away from her at terrific speed and she was flung face downwards in the hot, black sand. The second tremor had arrived. And just as suddenly it was gone.

It was several minutes before she dared to open her eyes. In the aftermath there was silence until a flock of crazed birds burst noisily from the trees and soared into the sky. Then nothing. Two trees had fallen, felled like saplings, and the sun shone through a dust cloud which hung over them as they settled. She was afraid to move.

The sand was burning her legs and she sat up gingerly, still with the sensation of the ground moving beneath her, but everything was motionless, suspended in time. The hut behind her was not too badly damaged. Part of one wall had collapsed and the roof was tiptilted, giving the place a comical, drunken appearance. Minella gave a spontaneous giggle. She was a great believer in the power of prayer, but never had one been answered so quickly, or so dramatically.

But when she looked at the trees all humour vanished. If she had continued running she would have been crushed under the nearest one. If Vasco hadn't shouted. . . .

Vasco! She strained her ears for any sound, but there was none. She couldn't have imagined his voice calling her. That was stretching miracles a bit far. He had been coming to let her out of the hut when the first tremor struck, and his warning had saved her life. Oh, God, where was he now?

She struggled to her feet, stunned by the way fear had been replaced by greater fear. A short time ago she could have cheerfully strangled Vasco, but he had more than compensated for the way he had treated her earlier, and anger was forgotten. She had been equally to blame for what had happened at the hut, and it served her right for making her request to visit it sound like an invitation. Not that she had meant it to for a minute, but Vasco was impressionable and his pride had been hurt. He had needed time to cool off. And now he must be lying injured somewhere on the other side of that barrier of trees. She had to find him.

'Vasco! Vasco, where are you?' Her voice splintered the silence.

She ran to the trees and started climbing among the dense branches. The first one was lying over a narrow fissure that had opened up above the shore line and as she clambered on it she disturbed the delicate balance. It rolled sideways, tipping her off, and she landed back on the ground, trembling with shock. She felt as if she was in some cruel obstacle race with defeat at every turn and it would have been easy to give way to useless tears. She fought them back, digging her fingers painfully into her temples, and tried to breath slowly to calm herself.

'It's all right, Sparrow. You're safe now.'

It was Sam who picked her up. He had appeared out of nowhere. Drawing her gently to her feet, he folded her deep within his strong arms and murmured words of comfort to ease her agitation. One hand cupped the back of her head and massaged the tension spot at the nape of her neck with sensitive fingers until spasms of trembling became less severe. His mouth was against her hair.

'It's all right, my darling,' he whispered. 'It's all over.'

She thought she must be dreaming. The tender words in that soft, heart-melting voice washed over her like a soothing balm and she closed her eyes with exquisite relief. The feel of him against her brought intense pleasure to every susceptible part of her body. She was entranced. Then he held her at arms length and there was an unbearable sadness in his eyes which held her bemused until his face was so close to hers she was aware only of his mouth within a hair's breadth of her own. Her lips quivered as he touched them, exploring hesitantly, and she lost all sense of time and place. Her fingers found his hair, working upwards through thick, untidy curls to press into his scalp with catlike ecstasy. There had never been anything so perfect as that kiss given in the aftermath of fear and danger.

It was the reminder of danger that made her remember Vasco and she dragged her mouth away from Sam's, twisting out of his arms before delirium made her forget completely. Later on, if these moments were reality, they could discover each other anew, but first Vasco had to be found.

'Sam, we've got to look for Vasco,' she said desperately. 'He shouted to me just before the trees fell and I'm terrified he might be trapped somewhere.'

Sam gave his head a shake, as if to clear it, and his eyes hardened. He straightened his back.

'Vasco is in the cottage being looked after by your brother and Annette,' he said. 'He didn't shout to you . . . I did.'

His voice was cool now, unemotional, and there was censure in the peremptory tone.

'Oh, Sam. . . .' she faltered, bewildered by the sequence of events. 'How did you get here? And what happened to Vasco? Is he hurt badly? Was it the earthquake?'

He permitted himself a smile. 'Would you like me to answer that string of questions one at a time, or shall I relieve your mind first by telling you your boy-friend will survive?'

'He isn't my boy-friend. . . .'

Sam put his hands on his hips and scrutinised her sternly from under lowered brows. 'Look, Minella, I'm not entering into any discussion. We all have lovers' quarrels and get over them. Vasco told us what happened and I understand, so let's leave it at that.'

He turned abruptly and started walking up towards the thickest part of the grove, but Minella darted after him, grabbing his arm.

'No, we will *not* leave it at that!' she stormed. 'I want to know what he told you, and what you think you understand.'

Vasco had a lot to answer for, and wrong impressions had to be put right before there were any serious misunderstandings. Or was it too late? One look at Sam's face and her heart sank. He stopped again and gave her his full attention.

'We none of us act very wisely when we let our emotions run away with us, Sparrow,' he said. 'I can't condemn you for ignoring my warning about Vasco Hernandez. He must be an attractive young man to someone your age. When I found you together on my boat I blamed him entirely, but perhaps I was being unfair now I realise you both wanted to be alone. And I'm sorry your plans went wrong today, but you could at least have bothered to tell us you were going out with Vasco and we would all have been spared a few worrying hours.'

'You don't know anything about my plans,' she protested. 'And if you've been listening to Vasco you really have got the wrong end of the stick. I had a special reason for wanting to come here. . . .'

She broke off, checking the explanation that would have followed before any harm was done, because he mustn't know she had been prying into his past life. Luckily he wasn't curious.

'Excuses aren't necessary,' he said coldly. 'You're old enough to be responsible for your own actions, and it was only natural you should want to spend your last day on the island with someone you . . . are fond of. I'm not angry with you for your choice of companion, however misplaced I may think it, but the way you disappeared without a word was inconsiderate. Annette was worried sick when you couldn't be found.'

So that was it! The reason for his beastly mood was that Annette had been upset. Well, three cheers! It didn't matter any more what conclusions he had reached about her relationship with Vasco, she thought bitterly. He wore his tough, steely look as he categorised her, and he could go on thinking what he liked. The sooner she was back home in England and everything was normal again, the better it would be.

'How did you know where to find me?' she asked. 'Did you immediately think of your little love nest by the lake?'

The barb was unkind and his eyes narrowed even further. Oh, Sam, she cried inwardly. What were they doing quarrelling? She wasn't going to see him any more and she loved him so much, yet here they were having another slanging match and wasting precious time. If only he felt as she did! If only the clock could be turned back to that day on the boat when she had almost told him that she loved him; that beautiful, golden day just before Annette came back into his life. He would have laughed, of course, but at least he would have known.

It was no surprise to her when she admitted that love to herself once more. It had gone on just the same even when she had tried to shut him out of her thoughts and find fault with him. It would always be with her, but obviously Annette was the only woman he had ever cared for deeply and it remained to be seen what the future held for them both. She must just hope Sam Stafford would fade out of their lives again after tomorrow and they could all rest easy.

'Your brother searched round the harbour and Annette tried the shops,' he was saying, ignoring her last remark. 'Then by chance Henrique Porva phoned me and said he'd seen you with Vasco. From then I had a good idea where you'd gone, though I could hardly credit it. I suppose this is an ideal place to bring a lover, but I've only ever lived here alone until the day you were brought here against my will and completely disrupted everything.'

Minella pressed her lips together, remembering all that he had done for her in spite of his initial objections.

'Oh, Sam, I'm sorry,' she began.

'You don't have to be,' he said. 'No experience is

wasted in this world, and though you may not realise it you've taught me a lot.'

Her eyes widened with pleasure, incredulous that this self-reliant man could learn anything from her. 'Have I? Have I really?'

'Oh, yes.' He stroked his beard thoughtfully, and the iciness in his eyes melted. 'I've grown ... fond of you, Sparrow. When I felt that first tremor and knew you were down here I couldn't get to you quick enough. There's always a second wave about forty seconds later, and you were running straight into the trees. I was petrified!'

His gaze lingered on her, and though she was conscious of being dust-streaked and dishevelled it was irrelevant. She came closer to him, drawn by a magnetism too powerful to resist, and unable to look anywhere except into his eyes. In another second she would have fallen into his arms, her legs too weak to support her, but the charged moment was shattered by a shout from the other side of the trees.

'Sam! Sam, have you found Minella?' It was Annette. 'Vasco's nearly demented! Is she hurt?'

Sam turned instantly, a smile that she could only interpret as relief lifting the corners of his mouth.

'It's all right, Anne, we're coming!' he called, and went to take hold of Minella's hand, but she snatched it away.

'Wait,' she said. 'First tell me what happened to Vasco.'

The smile deepened as Sam looked at her with derisive amusement. 'When you went cold on him he was pretty furious, as you know,' he said. 'It isn't on, Minella, to lead a poor chap on like that and then change your mind, particularly one as impetuous as Vasco. He got his motorbike and scorched off for a ride round until you'd had time to come to your senses, but he was so preoccupied he drove into the back of an ox-cart and landed up in a pile of straw. Unfortunately he sprained his ankle and we came across him hobbling back to the cottage, pushing the motorbike. I didn't think he'd ever forgive you, but it sounds as if he might have done.'

Minella had started to walk alongside him, but she stopped in her tracks.

'Oh!' she cried, her eyes growing wide with exasperation. Then she remembered how she had felt about Vasco when he turned the key on her and a triumphant smile lit her face. 'It just serves him right!'

CHAPTER ELEVEN

MINELLA stood gloomily among the brass fenders, books and bric-à-brac on display in the Brighton antique shop that belonged to her brother, her mood matching the cold, damp November day. Only five months had passed since their return from the Azores. It felt like five years.

She had never had the same interest in antiques as Greg or Annette, but she knew enough about them to be left in charge of the shop on the odd times when both had to be away, and this was one of them. They were attending an auction in London, but with summer gone, taking the majority of tourists with it, there was very little to do, and since she got back Minella had needed to keep busy. It was the only way she could stop thinking about Sam.

He would have forgotten her by now. A man like Sam would shrug off an interlude with a troublesome girl who had been foisted on him, as if it had never happened. Maybe he had enjoyed the harmless attraction between them while it had lasted, but she could imagine him giving a cynical smile if he realised how she had almost fallen for it.

Almost! Thank goodness he had never known just how hopelessly she had fallen in love with him. He would probably laugh out loud. She felt wretched, the ache of parting hardly lessened since that morning at the airport when she had had to put on an act until goodbyes were said, otherwise she would have burst into uncontrollable tears.

Greg hadn't helped much. On the night before they left he had verbally torn her apart for making such a nuisance of herself.

'You should be ashamed, Minella,' he had said, having followed her to her room as soon as they were back at the house. 'Apart from anything else you ought to have had more sense than to trust a boy like that. It was thoroughly irresponsible. And to go off without a word to anyone was disgraceful!'

'I didn't intend to be long,' she explained. 'You were all at siesta and I would have been back before you missed me if Vasco hadn't jumped to all the wrong conclusions. Honestly, Greg, it wasn't what everyone seems to think.'

She hadn't seen her brother so angry for years, and it upset her badly.

'Sam is the one you must apologise to,' he went on. 'That man has gone out of his way to make us welcome. You'd think he'd known us for years, and you show him no gratitude. You amaze me!'

'Really!' she cried. 'And wasn't it *you* who objected so strongly when you saw me come out of his room one night? Make up your mind, Greg. Am I to show him gratitude, or would you rather I indulged in an innocent escapade with Vasco Hernandez?'

Greg's face coloured and he looked down at the carpet, shifting his feet uneasily. 'That wasn't what I meant and you know it. Now I know Sam better I'm sure I misjudged you that night.'

'How old-fashioned!'

'There's no need for sarcasm. All right, I know how it sounded, but I've got used to the idea of seeing the two of you together and I wouldn't mind if you decided to make it permanent. Sam would be good for you, calm you down, but I guess today's episode has put paid to that.'

'There was nothing to put paid to in the first place,' she had said adamantly, and went on to persuade him it was the worst possible idea. But her heart had been breaking. When Sam had kissed both girls at the airport, lingering slightly longer with Minella and teasing her with an affectionate smile, it was as much as she could do to keep from throwing herself into his arms.

And now all she had was memories. She stared out of the window, wondering whether she would ever be able to recapture the high spirits she had been noted for before joining the crew of the *Delphine Rose*. She had seen the yacht in harbour quite often since and viewed it with mixed feelings. With the help of a storm, the *Delphine Rose* had despatched her unceremoniously into Sam Stafford's life, and there were times when she thought it was the worst thing that could have happened. If she had never come in contact with him she wouldn't be suffering like this now.

The day was cold and a sea mist rolled in to obscure what sun there had been earlier, bringing dampness to everything. It dripped from the shutters and came against the window like fine rain. Even the brasswork all around had a dull bloom and she switched on an extra lamp to cheer things up a bit. Minella hated the cold, and in this weather the shop was positively depressing. She cinched a wine-coloured mohair cardigan tighter round her waist with a black suede belt that matched her boots, and a pleated tartan skirt swirled round her legs as she went through to the office at the back in search of comparative comfort until it was lunchtime, when she would be able to go for a walk along the sea-front. How on earth did Greg put up with this dismal place day after day? One morning was bad enough.

She switched on the gas fire and sat in front of it, her thoughts winging as always to the warm summer days on Fayal. She pictured the house in Horta with its random stonework and the smooth white panel between ground and first floor windows; the cottage with vines growing over the side wall; the garden and the bougainvillaea-covered fence. She thought of windmills and blue hydrangeas, and when she remembered the squeaking ox-cart wheels she thought of Vasco's unrepentant expression when they left him with Dr Porva to have his ankle attended to. And then, inevitably, she was back with Sam.

Would she ever be free of him? Since returning home she had withdrawn into a shell of reserve and was only really happy when she was out alone in her boat. She had gained promotion at work, and a new young man with the firm who had high ambitions kept trying to date her, calling her a mystery girl because she never talked about herself, but she wouldn't go out with him. She didn't want any dates yet, in spite of having bought herself a more sophisticated collection of clothes.

At first she had avoided all discussion about events on Fayal, thinking that it was better not to even mention Sam in case it caused any repercussions between Greg and Annette. She dreaded that more than anything. But Annette knew it was not only the trauma she had been through in the summer that was affecting Minella. Trusting her feminine intuition, she had invited herself to supper at Minella's flat one evening on the pretext of being lonely while Greg was at a meeting, and had gradually managed to bring the conversation round to Sam. They had been home about a month by then.

'I know I went on a bit that day in Ponta Delgada,' she said, having reminisced about the lovely time they had spent there. 'I've thought about it a lot since and I'm afraid I said some pretty rotten things. You really *did* fall in love with Sam, didn't you?'

Minella was taken unawares. She was so surprised at the sudden mention of his name her heart began to pound and she hadn't time to wonder what had brought about the observation.

'Yes, I loved him,' she admitted. What use denying it?

Annette's heart ached, too, for the way her husband's little sister had grown up since she met Sam Stafford. There was a new maturity about her, a quieter outlook on things generally, and the candid answer she gave showed a new acceptance of life's knocks. Resignation at the futility of such a love hadn't come easily.

'There's something you should know, Minella,' Annette went on. 'It might help you to get over it quicker, and if I'd had the courage I would have told you before.' She sat close to the younger girl, fondness for her very much in evidence. 'Do you remember me telling you once about the man I was going to marry before I met Greg?'

Minella smiled. 'He let you down, disappeared, behaved despicably. Yes, you told me everything about him except his name. And you didn't warn me *I* might fall into the same trap.'

'You knew!' Annette gasped.

'Not straight away. Not when we had that awful row at the hotel in Ponta Delgada. It was Vasco who recognised you from a portrait.' Minella paused, her eyes full of sympathy. 'Oh, Annette, it must have been dreadful for you!'

'It was,' Annette agreed. 'I wanted to tell Greg straight away, but somehow I kept avoiding it, and then it was too late. I had to risk the danger of meeting Sam again. But it didn't take me long to realise the old excitement wasn't there any more. He's changed, Minella. We both have, and though I felt a sort of nostalgic affection for him, I wouldn't swap him for Greg. After we got back I confessed it all to him, so he knows about it now and everything's fine. I'm only sorry *you* had to be hurt.'

'Don't worry, I'll get over it eventually. I'm not the sort to hanker long after a lost cause.'

Annette sighed, wishing there was something she could do, but she knew from experience that only time would help.

'It's a pity he didn't feel the same way,' she said, 'though I suppose he was a bit old for you. It would have been nice having him part of the family, but he told me that day at the hospital that there was someone else he was in love with.'

Oh, yes, thought Minella sadly, the truth of it was Sam still loved Annette, though it was a point in his favour if he hadn't let her know. And it was a weight off her mind to know that Annette only wanted Greg.

'Thanks for telling me anyway,' she said. 'It makes me feel a bit better.'

'That's what I hoped. You're not alone, Minella. We're here, and we love you. Never forget that.'

'I won't,' Minella promised.

Talking had helped a lot, and the days were not quite so long afterwards, but though she managed to appear more like her usual bright self for Greg's benefit, even perhaps reassuring Annette, there were still days when memories of Sam and his island were too painful to dwell upon. Minella was never sure if sunny weather or wet days were the worst, but certainly this particular morning had set her in the dumps with a vengeance.

She didn't like the shop at all. It bored her because she couldn't bear being so inactive, and she didn't care for the musty smell or the constant reminder of age and the degeneration it brought. Things over which Greg enthused often looked too old for a second glance, and she couldn't understand their value. Her flat was light and airy, and she wouldn't have wanted any of these things cluttering it up. She got up and flicked a duster over a depressingly dull oil painting which bore a three-figure price tag and decided she would rather live with one of Sam's awful pictures. For a few minutes she indulged in a longing to be back in the Azores that almost reduced her to tears; then she took herself to task. Nothing in life stood still, and there was certainly no going back. Once and for all she must stop thinking about what was gone and concentrate on the future. Tomorrow she would smile at the boy in the office who kept trying his luck, and she'd fix a date with him. She'd been alone too long.

Still wielding the duster, she came to a pile of old books in the corner and set about cleaning them up one at a time. Books were the most interesting things in the shop to Minella, and it wasn't long before she was flicking through them, studying the coloured plates in a collection of old horticultural volumes Greg had recently bought. When she came to one about pineapple growing she drew in her breath sharply. Of all the subjects to stumble upon today! She picked it up hesitantly, almost afraid to be reminded of that wonderful afternoon with Alban da Costa who had explained all about pineapples, and mistaken her for Sam's intended wife. How happy she had been!

She took the book over to the chair by the fire and soon became absorbed in it. There was so much fascinating information, and even though it had been written many years ago she could see the basic facts were the same. The subject was so engrossing she even delayed making coffee, and when the shop bell rang, announcing a customer, she put the book down reluctantly, hoping she could return to it quickly.

There was a man in the shop with his back to her, handling a piece of Bristol glass. Something about the way he stood, legs astride, shoulders well back, made Minella pause before approaching him, and she chided herself for letting the atmosphere of the pineapple book play tricks with her imagination. How many times since the summer had she seen men who resembled Sam in one way or another? She was getting used to the familiar lurch her heart gave just before she made the same mistake again, but this time it refused to be quietened. He was so tall his dark curly hair touched the chandelier and set the crystal tinkling as he turned. He put up his hand to steady it anxiously, and Minella's hands flew to her face, not with any concern for the chandelier, but because she couldn't believe her eyes.

It really was him.

'Sam!' she breathed.

He put down the blue glass and smiled calmly, then came over to her with outstretched hands. She put her own into them and they were lost within the strong grasp.

'Hello, Minella. I hope you're pleased to see me,' he said, looking down at her from his vast height which seemed magnified in the confined space.

She couldn't speak. Her lips parted and she tried to find words, but none came. He looked so different in a superbly tailored grey suit, a white shirt that emphasised his tanned skin, and grey silk tie. He appeared to be every inch a man who held authority and she was filled with awe.

'Oh, what a wonderful surprise!' she managed to say at last.

'I hoped you would think so.'

The coldness of the shop made her shiver and she longed to give him a warmer welcome in every way, but he was a stranger. She'd had no warning. What would he think if she flung her arms round him and pressed herself close? She tucked a strand of hair nervously behind her ear and tried to compose herself.

'I wish you'd phoned first,' she said. 'You've chosen the wrong day. Annette has gone to London with Greg, and there's only me here.'

Of course, he had come intending to see Annette. He'd never stopped loving her, so it was only natural he would try to see her as soon as he got back to England. She drew herself up straighter and lifted her chin, determined not to let him see her agitation.

'It was *you* I came to see,' said Sam. 'I went to the company where you normally work and they said you were here looking after the shop for the day.' His eyes were bluer than she remembered and they searched her face curiously. 'What made you think I'd want to visit anyone else first?'

'I automatically assumed. . . .' she faltered. 'You came to the shop. . . .'

He put a finger under the dignified chin. 'Never assume anything about me, Minella. I came to invite you out to lunch, but if you're in charge of this mausoleum I guess it'll be difficult.'

She giggled. '*You* don't like it either. I *am* glad—I thought it was just me.' And yet with Sam standing there the place was charged with new life. He brought a vibrance that transmitted itself to every nerve in her body and she was just as aware of him as she had always been. 'You really did arrive at an extraordinary moment. I was reading a book about pineapples, would you believe.' She looked at her watch. 'I can lock up for an hour at one o'clock. Can you wait until then?'

'I've waited five months to see you. No doubt I'll survive another hour,' he said. 'I'll pick you up later.'

Minella stared at the door after he had gone, and felt dizzy. She was tingling with excitement, her eyes shining, and she couldn't remember the last time she had felt so lightheaded. She would have to calm down. The lunch date would be a very civilised meeting between two people who had once been thrown together by a strange twist of fate, and after the reminiscences were done they would go their separate ways again. It would be wrong to read anything else into Sam's visit, although he had sounded genuinely anxious to find her.

Two people came in the shop with the declared intention of browsing. She left them to it and was surprised when they actually bought an expensive paperweight. Things were looking up! When they had gone she hugged herself, bubbling over with anticipation, and she kept repeating Sam's name out loud just to make sure she hadn't dreamt he'd come. A grandfather clock ticked with monotonous precision, its deep tone drumming in her ears at half the speed of her heartbeats, and each minute seemed longer than the last. An hour had never gone so slowly.

He was there promptly at one, at the wheel of a large hired car.

The grey suit gave him an elegant, citified appearance

she found hard to associate with him, and she was glad she had worn something suitable for lunch with this impressive stranger. She would behave with the utmost decorum, not a word out of place, and he would see the difference in her. The girl on the island had been only a creature of circumstance.

She locked the shop door, put the key away safely and tucked the black suede clutch bag under her arm. Her hair had been styled only yesterday and flicked away from her face with flattering highlights. Carefully applied eye make-up emphasised the size and soft colour of her eyes, and the colour on her cheeks contoured her lovely oval face, making it glow with fresh beauty on that cold wintry day. The high heels of her suede boots completed her feeling of confidence, and when Sam got out of the car and opened the door on the other side for her, as he had once done for Consuelo, Minella knew she had passed the test.

He took her to the hotel where he was staying, one of the largest along the sea-front, and invited her to choose from the sumptuous menu, which she did with aplomb. The wine was his choice, and he touched her glass with his in formal greeting, his eyes registering approval of her at the opposite side of the table. They were sitting by the window and the only colour outside came from umbrellas tilted against the heavy sea mist.

'You must find it cold here after Fayal,' she said. 'Are you planning to stay long?'

'I hope to be back there for Christmas, if everything turns out as I want it to.'

'You're here on business, then?'

He hesitated. 'You could say that.'

Over lunch they talked of mundane things, stilted conversation which led nowhere, and disillusionment began to set in. Minella didn't particularly like this other Sam Stafford who knew his way around and had waiters hovering over him, taking orders which he gave with autocratic detachment. He treated Minella with deference, giving her his full attention, yet there was something illusive about him, a watchfulness she didn't understand, and she felt she wanted to shake him out of it.

'Tell me,' she said, when polite trivialities were almost exhausted, 'how is Vasco Hernandez?'

Sam's lips twitched into a smile she recognised at last. 'He's very well. In fact he's getting married quite soon to a local girl Benita found to help with her father.' He paused, eyeing her quizzically. 'Perhaps it's just as well you dashed his hopes, Minella. He certainly wouldn't know how to cope with the sophisticated young woman I'm having the pleasure of entertaining right now.'

She wondered if he was teasing, but there was no hint of it, and she realised he was finding this meeting equally difficult. The old familiarity was behind them and both were confronted with new images they hadn't expected. It gave her satisfaction to know he respected it, but she sighed for the battles she had dared to wage with him in the past.

'I owe you an apology, Minella,' he went on. 'Vasco told me the truth about that day he locked you in the hut.' He smiled broadly and his eyes shone with amusement. 'I must say I'd have been inclined to do the same if you'd asked me to take you to a deserted cottage and it turned out you only wanted to see a picture.'

'So you know about that,' she said warily.

He became serious again. 'Why didn't you ask me about it?' he wanted to know.

He had put her in a spot. She wasn't sure how much to admit to knowing without involving them in discussion about Annette that might infringe on the present. She preferred to know nothing about his intentions in that direction.

'Vasco saw Annette and recognised the portrait,' she said. 'All I wanted to do was confirm that he was right.

I hadn't realised you and Annette had known each other previously. It was rather a shock.'

'I'm sure it was,' said Sam. He was looking at her keenly. 'It was a shock to me when she arrived at the airport, and she had the advantage. She'd already guessed it was me when she heard my name before she came to Fayal, but she begged me not to let on. It was silly of her. There was no reason why Greg shouldn't know we were once engaged. It happened a long time ago, and wouldn't make any difference to her marriage. Greg is far too sensible, but that's the way she wanted it.'

'And you still love her,' said Minella.

His glance became withering. 'My dear girl, what Annette and I feel for each other now is affection for old times' sake. I admit I was hypnotised when I first saw her, but it meant nothing. I'm afraid I let her down badly in the past and I'm not proud of it, but thank goodness she found it in her heart to forgive me.'

Minella looked out of the window at a group of people jumping down one at a time on to the beach and running down to the sea, regardless of the weather. It felt wrong being here in this luxury hotel with Sam. Neither of them belonged in this setting, no matter how conforming they appeared to be on the surface. His hands were better suited to the wheel of his powerboat than to the elegant silver cutlery. She had a brief mental picture of him in the cockpit of the *Samanne*, the wind tearing through his hair, billowing his open-necked shirt, and a surge of reawakened excitement stirred her blood.

'That portrait of Annette was the best painting you've ever done,' she said. 'You must have loved her very much when you did it. How could you possibly walk out on her?'

He gave an unexpected hoot of laughter and tipped back his chair. The waiter collected their dishes before bringing the sweet trolley, and precious minutes passed before she found out why he found it funny.

'Oh, Minella,' he said, now leaning towards her, 'I didn't paint that picture. My mother did, and she was rather a famous portrait painter. I value it greatly, as much for its artistic merit as anything.' He paused. Then: 'I only once did anything resembling a portrait. It was of you, the morning I carried you like a drowned bird up to Henrique Porva's. I wanted to capture that moment. One day I'll show it to you.'

Something in his voice made her catch her breath, an intimacy she hadn't heard before, and it was like music. One day, he had said. He was hoping to see her again after this rather impersonal reunion, but she was aware of a certain trepidation. He was feeling his way carefully, as if unsure of her, and it gave her confidence because he had never chosen his words with her before. But if their friendship was to develop they had to be honest with each other.

'Sam,' she said slowly, looking down at the cloth where fine crumbs were scattered. 'I found something else that day when I saw the portrait. It fell when I was getting it from the shelf and the back came loose. There was a newspaper cutting about you tucked inside.'

He was a long time replying, and she glanced up anxiously. His eyes were clouded with memories and she could see that for some reason they were painful. She almost wished she'd said nothing, but it was silly to go on pretending ignorance.

'I guessed you'd read it,' he said, 'and I'm glad you did. I thought perhaps Annette might have told you something about me, but I don't think she likes to remember I always put my job first.' He poured more wine. 'My work came before everything, Minella, and I couldn't really consider marriage while I was involved with danger and I kept putting it off. Then came the famous shooting incident and I copped it in the knee. They were going to have to amputate, but thank God I was spared that. The only trouble was I was told then that I was medically unfit to carry on with my original task and it had to be a desk job or nothing. I went to pieces. I'd always lived by my strength and my wits, and I couldn't face a static indoor existence, nor would my pride let me turn to Annette for help. I can see now I didn't love her enough. So I packed it all in, made a clean break and started afresh out in the Azores, determined to prove that I was still fit for anything. I took up bull-chasing because it was the most strenuous exercise I could find and I proved my strength was in no way diminished. I think at the back of my mind I eventually intented to apply for my old job again, but somehow the magic of the islands took over. It's a long time now since I hankered after the kind of excitement I used to know. I wouldn't go back now.'

Minella said nothing for a moment. He was looking at her closely, as if afraid she would challenge his decision, but nothing was further from her thoughts.

Then she said: 'I'm glad, Sam. I don't think I'd be happy knowing you'd taken up police work again.'

He relaxed visibly and a smile crept to the corners of his mouth again. 'There's no fear of it, I assure you. I've too many plans to work on when I get home to Fayal. Do you want to hear about them?'

'Yes, I do,' said Minella.

'Then let's get out of here.'

He signalled to the waiter, had the lunch charged to his account, and helped her on with the trench coat she had had the sense to bring with her. When they were outside on the hotel steps he stretched his neck uncomfortably and pulled at his tie.

'Do you mind if I take this damned thing off? It's nearly choking me!'

She laughed. 'I wish you would. It doesn't look right.'

With his shirt open at the neck he looked more like the man she loved, and she wished she dared slip her hand into his, but he was still a rather formidable figure, his height and good looks making him conspicuous enough for people to stare.

The mist was patchy now and a watery sun attempted to disperse it altogether but hadn't the strength. They crossed over to the promenade and crunched through shingle thrown up by an exceptionally high tide, and without either saying a word they sought the beach at the first access point. It was low tide.

'What are you doing this evening, Minella?' Sam called, as she darted ahead of him and climbed on to a low breakwater with tomboyish disregard for her clothes.

'I usually curl up with a good book,' she said.

'No special boy-friend that I don't know about?'

'None.'

She balanced on the slippery wood like a tightrope walker, handbag held aloft, and gazed out to sea with a strange wistfulness, as if her destiny was held in those grey rolling breakers. And then she smiled to herself. The sea had once swept her literally into Sam Stafford's arms. No wonder it brought nostalgia! She watched him pick up a stone and send it skimming across the water. He was the most wonderful, exciting man in all the world and she would never tire of feasting her eyes on him, but she could have cried at her own inadequacy. He was fond of her. He might even have had a sentimental wish to see her again while he was in England, but nothing more. She mustn't kid herself. But the sudden aching longing for him was worse than anything she had ever known and she closed her eyes momentarily against the pain. It was in that second she lost her balance. She hadn't realised she had gone too far along the breakwater until she landed in the waves with a frantic yell. Fortunately she was still upright, but the water reached her knees and she could feel the pull of the receding tide.

And all Sam Stafford did was laugh.

'Sam! Get me out of here!' she cried, struggling

against the suction of the shingle and getting more and more wet. 'Damn you, Sam, don't just stand there!'

Still roaring with laughter, he waited until she was near enough to grasp his outstretched hand, then jerked her clear of the water, and into his arms.

'Oh, Minella, my darling little Sparrow, that's the best thing that's happened today,' he told her.

She was shaking with temper because he found it so funny, and pummelled his chest with her fists.

'I don't know why you should think so. The water was freezing cold, and I've ruined my boots!'

'But it's proved you're the same scatterbrained girl I fell in love with. I was so afraid she'd been replaced by a gorgeous young career woman who would never put a foot wrong.'

'I am *not* a scatterbrain!' she protested loudly—then checked herself, convinced she hadn't heard him right. Her heart juggled with so many overwhelming emotions at once she felt sure he must hear the commotion it made, and she took a gulping breath. 'What did you say?'

He looked down at her, his eyes caressing every line of her face.

'I love you,' he said, very gently.

Her eyes widened with incredulous joy. 'Oh, Sam, I love you too!'

The simple declaration hung between them, spreading radiance with the blissful discovery; happiness so deep that further words were unnecessary. Time seemed suspended, and the sound of the breakers on the sand behind her was an orchestral accompaniment to the rapid beating of her heart. Then Sam kissed her. The touch of his mouth on hers was a sweetness so disturbing she seemed to merge as part of him.

'I knew you belonged to me from the moment I picked you up and held you in my arms,' he murmured. 'I've never been so strangely affected by anything, and I was afraid to take you to my house because I knew somehow that you were going to change my life. It was as if I'd been waiting for you since the day I was born. I can't explain. These months away from you have been unbearable, but I had to give you time to recover from all you'd been through. I couldn't expect you to decide anything rationally while you were still on the island. It wouldn't have been fair.'

'But I loved you then,' she said, 'from the first second I opened my eyes and saw you.' She paused. Her fingertips caressed his cheek and lingered against his lips while he kissed them. 'No, it was even before that. When you held me that morning there was a bond between us that didn't need words, and since then I've thought of no one but you.'

He smiled, remembering the way it had been. 'I felt it, too. I thought my island had everything I needed to make me happy, but as soon as I saw you I knew I would never be completely happy until you were sharing it with me. Say you'll marry me straight away and we can be there for Christmas.'

'No, Sam.' A shadow crossed her face. 'I must be with Greg at Christmas.'

'Then we'll make it a Christmas wedding. How about that? We'll discuss it over dinner at the hotel this evening.' He kissed her again before she could make another excuse, and the way she clung to him was his answer.

'Wonderful,' she agreed. 'But I've a better idea for this evening. I shall cook dinner for the two of us at my flat.'

He held her away from him, a wicked smile lighting his eyes and curving his mouth. 'Sparrow, if you're willing to be alone with me, knowing how much I want you, there's nothing I'd like better.'

She gave his beard a playful tug, then snuggled back into the warmth of his arms, hearing the way his heartbeats matched her own.

'I hate to shock you, Sam, but I want to be alone

with you so much I don't know how I'm going to live through the afternoon in that awful shop.'

'Tell you what,' he suggested, 'read as much as you can about pineapple growing, and bring the book with you this evening. We're going into business, my darling. I've already acquired the land and all I want now is a loving wife to share my enthusiasm.' He paused to stroke back some hair that was blowing into her eyes. 'Oh, Minella, we're going to have such a wonderful life together!'

Without more ado he picked her up in his arms, careless of the wet skirt and boots marking his city suit, and kissed her thoroughly before setting off up the beach with long, easy strides.

Harlequin® Plus

A WORD ABOUT THE AUTHOR

Pamela Pope can trace her ancestry back to the first duke of Suffolk, though her family's "blue blood" has been diluted by an assortment of interesting characters who have hovered in her mind, piquing her writer's imagination.

When she was a girl in Yorkshire, England, during World War II, she passed many long hours escaping the problems around her by writing stories. Though her friends loved the tales, her teachers were less enthusiastic, especially as Pamela persisted in her writing endeavors during Latin lessons. One of her efforts had to be rescued from the staff waste basket!

But it was real-life romance rather than romantic fiction that first claimed her when she grew up. She moved to the Isle of Wight and met her husband-to-be, a man who insists that theirs was love at first sight.

When her two daughters were born, Pamela began to take her writing more seriously than ever before. A trip abroad—to Mississippi—gave her the spark of inspiration she needed to begin her first romance novel. Now, with several books to her credit, she feels her writing career has brought exciting rewards — not just financial but personal, as well.

What romance fans say about Harlequin...

"...scintillating, heartwarming... a very important, integral part of mass-market literature."

—J.G.,* San Antonio, Texas

"...it is a pleasure to escape behind a Harlequin and go on a trip to a faraway country."

—B.J.M., Flint, Michigan

"Their wonderfully depicted settings make each and every one a joy to read."

—H.B., Jonesboro, Arkansas

*Names available on request.